Winter Escapes

Around the world in four romances!

Pack your bags and leave the postfestivity blues behind! This January, Harlequin Romance presents a whirlwind tour to some stunning international locations—and we want you to join us. Whether you're looking for sun, sea or snow, we've got you covered. So let yourself be swept away by these beautiful romances and discover how four couples make it to their true destination... happy-ever-after!

Get ready for the trip of a lifetime with...

Their Hawaiian Marriage Reunion
by Cara Colter

Copenhagen Escape with the Billionaire
by Sophie Pembroke

Prince's Proposal for the Canadian Cameras
by Nina Singh

Cinderella's Moroccan Midnight Kiss
by Nina Milne

All available now!

Dear Reader,

I've had the privilege of visiting Canada quite often, having grown up somewhat nearby. Toronto is one of my favorite cities to spend time in, and Montreal is so utterly charming regardless of the season. So I was beyond excited when the opportunity arose to write a story set in that lovely country. Raul and Sofia's romance is set against some of the most romantic regions on the planet. The two started out as friends in their youth and have been pining for each other ever since throughout the years. Though only one of them knew it! A fake relationship devised to draw the attention of the world turns all too real as they travel through amazing sites within Canada. I hope you enjoy their journey and their story.

Nina Singh

PRINCE'S PROPOSAL FOR THE CANADIAN CAMERAS

NINA SINGH

ROMANCE

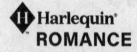

Harlequin®
ROMANCE

ISBN-13: 978-1-335-21627-4

Prince's Proposal for the Canadian Cameras

Copyright © 2025 by Nilay Nina Singh

Recycling programs
for this product may
not exist in your area.

 Harlequin Enterprises ULC
22 Adelaide St. West, 41st Floor
Toronto, Ontario M5H 4E3, Canada
www.Harlequin.com

Printed in U.S.A.

Nina Singh lives just outside Boston, Massachusetts, with her husband, children and a very rambunctious Yorkie. After several years in the corporate world, she finally followed the advice of family and friends to "give the writing a go, already." She's oh-so happy she did. When not at her keyboard, she likes to spend time on the tennis court or golf course. Or immersed in a good read.

Books by Nina Singh

Harlequin Romance

A Five-Star Family Reunion

Wearing His Ring till Christmas

How to Make a Wedding

From Tropical Fling to Forever

If the Fairy Tale Fits...

Part of His Royal World

From Wedding Fling to Baby Surprise
Around the World with the Millionaire
Whisked into the Billionaire's World
Caribbean Contract with Her Boss
Two Weeks to Tempt the Tycoon
The Prince's Safari Temptation
Their Accidental Marriage Deal
Bound by the Boss's Baby

Visit the Author Profile page
at Harlequin.com for more titles.

To my dear Pool Mon friends.
I am so very thankful for each of you.

CHAPTER ONE

THE CALL WOULD come in any minute now. Raul knew as soon as he woke up and was alerted by his assistant to check social media.

His father, the king, would be calling him the second he got wind of the information Raul had just seen.

And he would order Raul to fix it all. Tell him to clean up another mess his sister was responsible for. Again.

Her latest mistake was quite a doozy, he had to admit. Even by Luisa's standards. Of all the ways to bring unwanted scrutiny on the family name.

Raul barely had time to wipe the sleep out of his eyes when, sure enough, his phone began to vibrate and sound the alarm he had assigned to the king.

He picked it up with a sigh. "Your Highness."

"Why do you allow her to do such things?" his father immediately responded.

"Hello to you too, Father."

"When was the last time you saw your sister?" his father demanded to know, ignoring his greeting.

Before she started all this. Or at least that's what Raul thought. But there was no way to know for sure. Just as anything else involving Luisa, his guess was as good as anyone else's

"I'm not sure, Father," Raul answered, his voice a croak both from the grogginess of sleep as well as frustration.

"Well, you should. You know what happens when she's left to her own devices."

Raul sighed, turning away from the phone. "She's a grown adult, Father. I can't very well trail her throughout her travels and escapades."

"Well, you're the only one we even have a hope of getting her to listen to. She never did heed me or your mother. Never did."

How was that his fault exactly?

His father answered his unspoken question. "I would think you'd try harder to rein her in."

Raul pinched the bridge of his nose. He'd have better luck trying to control a lightning storm. He supposed he couldn't really blame his father for being upset. The way Luisa drew unwanted attention to the royal family with her antics would drive the most patient monk to anger. But this latest escapade of hers certainly topped all the others. So far.

"You are older and wiser, after all," his father added.

Hah! As if that was any kind of argument. He was older than Luisa by a whole fifteen months. Why everyone in the kingdom seemed to forget that was beyond him.

Raul sighed. He knew full well it wasn't even worth the effort to try to make that argument. It never worked.

"Just look at the links I've sent you. Those photos are downright scandalous."

Raul reached for his tablet and called up his father's latest texts, keeping the phone to his ear. Though he hardly needed to look at the sites the links led to. He could pretty much guess what he'd be seeing. Bingo. Pictures of his sister popped up on his screen. If she knew the cameras were focused on her, she didn't seem to care.

Luisa on a yacht in a barely-there bikini, laughing at her lover. Luisa dancing in a smoky nightclub, her married boyfriend holding her about the waist. The last one was particularly racy. Luisa and the man in a deeply passionate kiss against a backdrop of a sandy beach. His sister may as well have been topless given the tiny scrap of fabric that was her swim top. The captions were as tawdry as one would expect.

Raul tossed the tablet aside. Truth be told, he

was rather disappointed in Luisa himself. But his disappointment had nothing to do with his worry over salacious gossip. No. Rather, he'd thought higher of her character.

Luisa had always been a free spirit. A quality he'd actually admired and envied below the surface. Not that he would ever admit it. But she'd never been cruel or hurtful. Having a very public affair with a married man definitely qualified as being cruel. Particularly for the man's wife and children.

What in the world was she thinking?

What Luisa was doing ran far past reckless free-spiritedness.

The entire world was now having a field day with the salacious gossip. Not that Luisa cared two figs about what was said about her. But the king, well, he cared a lot. Making this whole fiasco somehow Raul's problem to solve.

"You know I can't convince Luisa to do anything she doesn't want to, Father." Even trying would have the opposite effect. His sister would only double down like a child who was being reprimanded.

"I know," the king said on a sigh so long and loud that Raul actually felt a trickle of concern. His father wasn't a young man. And he still insisted on performing his regular duties day in and day out. Any added stress wasn't good for his overall health. His doctor had already warned about the family history of various ailments his father had to watch for at his age. In fact, the king was the same age his own father, Raul's grandfather, had been when he'd suddenly and unexpectedly passed.

A shudder passed through Raul at the thought. As demanding as the king could be, he was still his father. He and Luisa had already lost one parent.

A selfish twinge of thought entered his mind. Losing his father was unbearable to contemplate. But there was something else. Raul was heir to the throne. As much responsibility as he already shouldered, he simply wasn't ready to be king just yet. The day would come soon enough. But he wanted to be more prepared.

Not to mention, the moment Raul ascended, the pressure to find a wife and procure an heir would be instantaneous. And he certainly wasn't nearly ready for any of that. Picking up his father's slack as he grew older and maintaining the investments he'd made to grow the kingdom's coffers was more than enough responsibility on him for now.

Raul swallowed a curse, pushing away the self-centered thought with no small amount of guilt. He redirected his attention back to his father on the other end of the line.

"Our only hope is to somehow take the world's attention off Luisa," his father said. "And onto something else."

"I guess we can hope for some kind of world-wide calamity," Raul quipped.

"Don't try to be cute," the king admonished. "You know that's not what I mean."

"Well, I have something of a tour coming up. That should count for something."

"That won't be enough," the king replied. "If anything, Luisa's affair will overshadow all your efforts. You'll constantly be dodging questions about your sister."

He had a point.

"Unless…"

Uh-oh. His father's tone and hesitation was uncharacteristically coy. Alarm prickled along the surface of Raul's skin. Whatever the king was about to say, Raul wasn't going to like it. Something told him any kind of distractive calamity was going to be personally not in his favor.

"Yes?" Raul asked, already dreading the possible answer. "Unless what?"

"Unless they were asking you questions about a much safer topic."

"Such as?" Raul asked.

Something told him his father's lips had widened into a smile. "You, son."

* * *

Sir Bunbun was hardly behaving in a gentle-manly manner this morning. Sofia Nomi wasn't quick enough and received yet another splash of water to her face and torso, which took her from somewhat damp to dripping wet. She bit down on a curse and wiped her cheeks with the back of her forearm.

The not-so-subtle giggle from her assistant and best friend did nothing to lighten her mood.

"Come on, Bunbun," Sofia coaxed. "The sooner you behave, the sooner we can get this bath over with."

"It's Sir Bunbun," Agnes corrected. "His mama was very clear that we are to use his full name. You don't want to offend him now, do you?"

Sofia could only manage a grunt in response as Sir Bunbun shifted in the large tub and gave her face a wet and sloppy lick.

"Ugh!"

That wasn't the worst of it. The Great Dane–Labrador mix chose that moment to jump on his hindquarters and slosh out half the water in the utility sink. He landed his front paws with a thud on her shoulders and gave her another lick.

Sofia sucked in a breath and summoned as much patience and calm as she could muster. It wasn't much.

"Don't you dare laugh, Agnes," she warned to no avail. Her friend had her palm cupped around her mouth in an unconvincing attempt to silence her continuing giggles.

"Sorry," Agnes said. "He's just such a goofy giant," she added, giving Bunbun an affectionate scritch behind one ear. "How about I go get some more towels? The next batch should be about done."

Sofia fervently hoped so. "That would be great. Thanks."

Nothing had gone right today. She'd arrived in the morning to find that the service who cleaned and prepped for her after-hours had hired a new employee who'd neglected to launder the service towels. Her first appointment had come in particularly filthy, then a walk-in had pled with her to handle her new puppy who'd had a run-in with a skunk this morning. Sofia had reluctantly given in because of the woman's tear-filled pleas. To fit the terrier in, she'd given up her regular half hour for lunch. Her stomach reminded her of that injustice with a loud, gnawing growl even as she had the thought. Now, Sir Bunbun was behaving particularly rambunctiously, even for him. Agnes was right about him being a gentle giant. But the giant part made grooming him an adventure in patience and stamina when he wasn't behaving.

It didn't help that she was operating on very little energy or stamina after such a restless night due to yet another disquieting phone call from Phil yesterday. Her stepfather could be persistent, in a most annoying way. She supposed he had to be to achieve his level of success as a Washington, DC, businessman. As grateful as she was that her mother had finally found someone who loved her and looked out for her, Sofia couldn't help but wish Mama might have married someone a bit less ambitious.

To make matters worse, Phil's latest scheme involved using *her* as a bargaining chip! The whole idea smacked of impropriety as far as Sofia was concerned. And if her mother wasn't so in love and was instead thinking clearly, she'd see it that way too.

Sofia gave her head a shake. She would have to deal with Phil and his impossible ask later. Right now she had to get Bunbun taken care of. "Why are you being so naughty?" she chided the dog. "You really ought to be better behaved, young man."

The canine tilted his head, as if trying to understand her. Sofia couldn't help but smile. Despite all his trouble, he really was a charmer. "How about we compromise, huh?" she asked, gently removing his paws from her shoulders and setting them back down into the utility sink.

"If you stop acting as you have been, I'll give you a special treat later. Our little secret," she whispered. "Just between you and me." Bunbun's mama could be a little strict with the treats. But honestly, for a dog his size, Sofia couldn't see the difference between one Graham Bone treat or two.

Sofia heard the sound of someone clearing their throat echoing from the front of the store.

"We'll be right with you," she shouted, wondering why there was anyone out there. Bunbun was her last appointment. And if it was another walk-in, Sofia would just have to put her foot down and tell the pet owner that another groom today was out of the question.

Where was Agnes? It couldn't possibly take her that long to pull towels out of the dryer.

"Perhaps you can come back tomorrow?" she shouted over the curtain. "This isn't a really great time."

"Sorry to hear that," came the response, carried on a deep, gravelly voice.

Sofia froze in the act of sponging Bunbun's haunch as a ripple of awareness ran over her skin. That voice. She would know it anywhere. But it couldn't be. Could it?

Agnes chose that moment to reappear carrying a mountainous stack of towels. Sofia grabbed the top one and began to dry her hands.

"Could you take over with Bunbun?" she asked, then turned around without waiting for an answer. She had to go see if her ears were deceiving her.

Sofia pulled the curtain to the side, trying to ignore the shaking in her hands. She had to be mistaken. There was no way Prince Raul Refik Abarra could possibly be standing in her little pet grooming shop.

"Hello, Sofia."

Sofia swallowed the brick that instantaneously formed at the base of her throat. If her ears had been deceiving her, her eyes were following along.

She somehow managed to make her mouth work. "Prince Raul. To what do I owe the honor?"

He winked at her. "No need to be so formal, Soso. It's me."

Raul wasn't expecting the figurative gut punch that struck when Sofia appeared from behind the dividing curtain. Funny, he didn't remember her being quite so…alluring. And how was that even possible, given her current state of disarray? She was soaking wet, her hair slipping out of the complicated topknot on her head and falling messily around her face.

Yet, despite her dishevelment, a surge of electricity shot through his core at the sight of her, heating him from within. Maybe he was just tired. Or suffering from some weird form of jet lag after his long flight.

"Um…what are you doing here?" she asked, clearly in shock.

"Sorry if I'm interrupting something." He'd clearly walked in when she was predisposed. Taking care of an animal. Though, for a split second when he'd first arrived and heard her words from behind the curtain, he'd thought perhaps he'd just walked in on some sort of foreplay.

A strange and unfamiliar sensation had washed over him when he'd heard her melodic voice uttering those words. A feeling he refused to believe might have bordered on jealousy. No, he'd simply felt a moment of alarm. This whole idea would be sorely hampered if Sofia was currently involved with someone. There was no plan B. His security had run a check and looked into the possibility, and assured Raul that she was single currently. Her last relationship had ended about a year ago. And it had been short enough that using the word *relationship* was a bit of a stretch.

Sofia dabbed the towel along her hairline, then lower down her neck. Raul had to resist the urge to ask her if he could take over the task.

Whoa. He really had no business thinking such thoughts. He was here for one reason. To ask her about a fake relationship. Emphasis on the *fake*. No real attraction allowed.

"I was just…uh…with a client," she said and gestured to her soaking apron. "He was less than cooperative, as you can see."

He nodded. "I heard too. I'm guessing the offer of a special treat did the trick?"

Was it his imagination or were her cheeks beginning to flush?

"Not as well as I'd hoped," she answered. "Bunbun was much more interested in licking me than the treats in my pockets, however."

Raul figured he couldn't really blame the beast. Sofia did indeed appear quite lickable.

Damn it.

Yet another wayward thought he had no business entertaining. What was wrong with him? He couldn't remember the last time he'd felt such attraction to a woman. On one hand, it would make all the pretending that much easier. On the other hand, however, it could complicate matters in so many ways.

First thing first. Sofia had to actually agree to his offer.

"Bunbun?" he asked, trying to focus on the mundane to quell the errant emotions coursing through him.

She nodded. "Sir Bunbun, actually. We were told to use his full name."

"I see." He gestured to the back. "Can I help you perhaps? With Sir Bunbun?" He had to suppress a chuckle at the ridiculous name.

She looked horrified at the idea. Her gaze traveled him from head to toe. "I don't think that's a good idea. I wouldn't let that suit anywhere near any of the animals back there, let alone a massive beast sitting in a tub full of water. I know for a fact that what you wear is custom-made and that suit probably costs as much as a foreign sports car."

She was right, though off by several thousand dollars. He could probably buy two sports cars for what it cost.

He shrugged. "No matter. I can help if you need."

She gave her head a shake, sending droplets of water flying through the air. "Thanks. But no. And surely you didn't come here to talk about my clientele or their misbehavior."

He gave her a small bow. "You're right. As interesting a topic as that is."

"So why are you here then?" she repeated. "Are you here on official business?"

He really didn't want to get into any of the reasons for his visit here in the middle of her shop, but he supposed he had to give her something. "Yes and no."

She blinked at him. "What does that mean exactly?"

"I'm here to see you."

More confused blinks, then her features softened. "Is this about Luisa?"

"In a sense."

She squinted at him, as if studying a new breed of canine she hadn't come across before. "'Yes and no. In a sense.'" She repeated his words, then repeated herself, "What does that mean exactly?"

A loud bark sounded from behind the curtain and echoed through the air.

"I am indeed here because of my sister. I'm sure you've heard the rumors."

Her lips tightened. "She called me, tried to explain."

"Well, there is no reasonable explanation for what she's doing as far as my father is concerned."

"The king."

He nodded. "Yes, he's very concerned about the negative attention this has brought on the royal family."

"I see. But I'm not sure why any of that would bring you here."

"You're in an ideal position to help us with it."

Another loud bark from the back drowned out his last word.

"Me? How can I help? Luisa's got her own mind. There's nothing I can say or do to convince her to stop doing something she wants to do."

He waited for another round of barking before speaking again. "That's not what I mean by having you help. And I'd like to explain fully. But at a better time and a quieter place." Bunbun barked once more as if to emphasize his point. "What time do you close up shop?"

"Around five thirty."

"Do you have any plans after?"

Her answer was a very slow shake of her head. "No plans. Unless you count soaking in a hot tub and slipping into bed to stream a show."

Darned if his mind didn't automatically picture her in that tub and then bed before he shook the image away.

"Excellent. I'll have a car pick you up around seven."

She rubbed a palm down her face as if taking it all in, not quite believing it. A tremor of guilt nagged at him. He really shouldn't have shown up unannounced. But up until literally an hour ago, he wasn't even actually sure he was ready to go through with any of this.

Now, there was no turning back.

CHAPTER TWO

HER DOORMAN RANG her at 7:00 p.m. on the dot. "There's a car here for you, Sofia."

"Coming, Frank."

Sofia took one last glance in the mirror and rubbed her palm down her midriff.

So this was actually happening. She hadn't imagined Raul in her shop a few hours ago. He really had been there. And in a few short minutes, she'd be meeting him for dinner.

Part of her still couldn't quite believe it. Her phone dinged with a text message as she strode to the door.

My driver should be there to pick you up. I look forward to our meeting. R

Meeting. For some reason the last word landed with a thud as she read it. How silly of her. Of course, that's all this was. Not like Raul had asked her out on some kind of date. The man was the Prince of Vesovia, for heaven's sake. So far out of Sofia's league, he may as well be in another dimension. He'd appeared so imposing and out of place in her modest little shop. The last time she'd seen him, he'd still been harboring the leftover features of a youthful teenager. The man who'd appeared at her shop was a fully mature male.

Raul still called her Soso. She knew it was simply gentle teasing that had carried over from their teen years, but the underlying message was clear. He thought her average, mediocre, just so-so. And who could blame him? The man was set to inherit an island kingdom in the not-so-distant future.

She bathed and trimmed pets for a living.

No. He was only here because of his sister. He'd told her that he wanted to speak to her about Luisa. That she could somehow help with the latest mess her friend had gotten herself involved with. Though for the life of her, she wasn't sure what she could possibly do. True, Sofia and Luisa had become close friends during their high school years. And they'd kept in touch off and on through the years. But Luisa was as headstrong as they came. If she wasn't listening to her brother or her own father, a man who happened to be a king, how in the world could Sofia get her to see reason about her taboo relationship?

She was still pondering that very question when she made her way downstairs and out of her building. The "car" Raul had sent was a shiny black stretch limousine. Complete with a tuxedoed driver who stood by the passenger door and opened it for her when she reached him.

How the man had maneuvered such a long vehicle through her tight NoMa street, she could simply marvel at. Within minutes they were driving past the Capitol Building toward the heart of the city. She wasn't even surprised when he finally pulled up to the swankiest hotel in the DC area and stopped the car. Sofia should have known this was the place they'd be having dinner. All the dignitaries and heads of state who visited DC stayed here. She'd expect nothing less from Prince Raul Abarra of Vesovia. Only the best. As befitting a future king.

Still, she couldn't help but feel a bit like a character in a fairy tale when a uniformed attendant immediately appeared to accompany her to the front entrance and through the lobby.

A girl could get used to this.

She followed the man through the extravagant lobby and to a set of steel elevator doors. Once inside, he retrieved a key card from his pocket and swiped it along a panel on the wall. The topmost button lit up and he pushed it with a well-manicured finger. Sofia actually felt the pressure change in her ears as they climbed up. How high were they going exactly?

She got her answer when the car finally slowed a few moments later and the door swished open. To the very top, it seemed, all the way to the rooftop. The attendant nodded to her with a smile and gestured for her to exit the car. She didn't even know this hotel had a rooftop dining option. It was probably one of the well-kept secrets of the DC that only certain people knew about. People like a crown prince.

Who happened to be the only one up here. Raul stood up from where he'd been sitting at a white-clothed table and immediately strode to greet her.

Sofia's breath hitched at the sight of him. In a dark suit jacket with a silk shirt unbuttoned at the top, Raul was breathtakingly handsome. His dark hair glistened amid the backdrop of the city lights behind him and the light of the full moon above. She thought she might have stepped into a cologne ad.

He dismissed the other man without so much as a word, merely a simple glance and an almost imperceptible nod, then took Sofia by the hand. A bolt of current shot through her arm at his touch and traveled through to her core.

She really had to get a grip. She wasn't the silly schoolgirl who had an embarrassing crush on her best friend's older brother anymore. She didn't have to react like a lovelorn fool at the simplest touch from the man.

"Thank you for agreeing to meet me, Sofia," Raul said and led her to the table he'd just left, then pulled a chair out for her. "And on such short notice."

Sofia glanced around at the other empty tables and chairs and realized that he must have arranged for them to have the entire restaurant to themselves.

"I'll have to admit, the curiosity was eating away at me about why you asked me here."

He didn't get a chance to answer as a gentleman appeared at their side and filled their glasses with an icy pitcher of water.

"I asked the chef to prepare a Mexican-themed menu for us this evening," Raul said after the man left. "I hope that's okay."

"That sounds great." Tacos were practically a staple of her diet. Though the ones prepared here were probably a far cry from her usual food truck stop outside her grooming shop.

Raul nodded then lifted his arm. A waitress appeared with two goblets full of golden liquid. She placed one in front of Sofia first. "Our custom recipe margarita, madame."

Sofia raised her hand. As tempting as the concoction looked, she was going to have to pass.

"You can have mine too. No drinks for me, I'm afraid," she told Raul after the woman left.

He lifted an eyebrow. "Oh? Why's that?"

"I have an early grooming appointment to-morrow. A poodle—they're a lot of work. And this one has to be perfect or I'll have the owner come back repeatedly until she gets her exactly how she wants her."

"Can't you delegate? It is your shop after all."

She shook her head. "There's only me and Agnes. And this poodle is a two-person job."

He took a sip of his drink and studied her. "No other employees."

Sofia resisted rolling her eyes. Imagine having to explain strict budgeting to a prince who never had to worry about finances.

"I'm afraid not. I'd love to hire more qualified people. I simply can't afford it."

Raul set his drink down and leveled a look toward her she couldn't quite place. Though it had the effect of making her quake inside. As if he was about to let her in on some secret that only he knew about.

"What if I told you I could help you with that? And more."

Sofia chuckled at the question. How much more curious could this possibly get? "And how exactly would you do that?"

She wasn't prepared in the least for his answer.

* * *

She couldn't possibly have heard him correctly. In fact, maybe none of this was actually happening. Maybe she wasn't even really here. Maybe Sir Bunbun had knocked her over this afternoon and she'd managed to fall and hit her head. Perhaps she was lying on the tiled floor of her shop right at this very moment having the most elaborate of dreams.

That theory made much more sense than what she thought she'd just heard.

"I see I've shocked you," coma-induced Raul said from across the table with surprising clarity for a figment of her imagination.

"I think I may have that drink after all."

Raul nodded in the direction of the waiting server, who immediately appeared with a fresh cocktail for her.

Sofia took a sip, then gave her head a brisk shake to try to clear her thoughts. "I'm sure I misheard you. Because I really thought you just said that you wanted to hire me as part of some PR scheme for the royal palace that involves me pretending to be your fiancée." She lifted her glass for another sip. "Which can't be correct, obviously. So, either I misheard, or I'm in a coma."

The corner of his mouth lifted ever so slightly.

"Those are the only two options you've come up with then?"

"They're the only ones that make a lick of sense."

Yet another waiter arrived with their food. He set a plate of empanadas that were still steaming in front of them and a serving tray with an array of sauces.

Sofia would have thought she was too distracted to eat, but her mouth watered at the aroma wafting through the air. She'd been way too tired and full of anticipation to have a snack after work despite having missed lunch. Now she realized she was starving. A loud growl sounded from the vicinity of her stomach to confirm.

Raul used the pair of tongs on a separate plate to lift an empanada and drop it on her plate. Then he took one for himself.

"Maybe we should eat first before we discuss the details. I'd prefer to do this on a full stomach."

"The details of what exactly?"

"Eat, Sofia. First thing first."

She held in a snicker. "As bossy as ever, I see." She wanted to take the words back as soon as they left her lips. That was no way to talk to royalty. What if she'd gone and offended him?

To her surprise, Raul merely chuckled in response, then popped the entire empanada in his mouth after dipping it in the thickest of the sauces. "I've told you the gist of the proposal. We'll get into the specifics once you get some food in you."

She took a forkful of her appetizer and chewed, studying him while he helped himself to another empanada.

Sofia leaned back in her chair. "Wait. So you're actually serious. About this fake-engagement idea."

He swallowed before nodding.

She put down her fork. "I'm sorry. I'm going to need you to explain sooner rather than later."

"Now who's the bossy one?"

She merely tapped her finger on the table impatiently.

"Look, this kind of thing isn't unheard-of," he began. "The fact of the matter is, Luisa is bringing a lot of scandalous attention to the royal family. The gossip has gotten out of control. My father asked me to create something of a distraction."

"By shifting all the focus on yourself."

"Correct. And in a positive way. You're the answer to it all."

"How so?"

He shrugged. "Simple. You just have to be seen with me. At three events in particular."

"What events?"

The first one right here in DC. The Washington Journalist Association dinner."

"The one with all the celebrities and politicians?"

"That's right."

"That's just three nights from now."

"I know."

Sofia inhaled a deep steadying breath. Her head was spinning. "What other events?"

"The next stop on my agenda is Canada."

Sofia practically jumped in her seat. "You want me to go to Canada with you?"

He nodded. "First stop is Toronto for a wedding. Then Montreal for the mayor's seasonal awards ball."

"Whose wedding?"

"Francesca Tate."

He had to be kidding. "*The* Francesca Tate? *That* wedding?"

"Correct."

That was the celebrity wedding of the decade. If not the century. Francesca Tate was a multi-award-winning actress known and adored the world over. And here was Raul, casually discussing taking Sofia to the event the whole world was anticipating as casually as a teenager asking to go get ice cream.

"Like I said. You're perfect as the fake fiancée who's accompanying me to it all."

If her skepticism were a tangible thing, it could take a seat at the table. "If you say so. One part of this I don't understand at all."

"What's that?"

"Why me? I mean, I'm hardly princess material."

She really didn't see it. Just how perfect she would be for what he had in mind. Sofia checked all the boxes—familiarity with the royal family, her devotion to his sister, nothing salacious in her past, a self-owned business. And she was beautiful to boot, that last part being an added bonus. He studied her now, the US Capitol Building looming in the distance behind her. Striking hazel eyes, hair the color of midnight. High cheekbones that were somehow always lush with color. Thick, full red lips.

Focus. She had asked him something.

"Well, first of all. You happen to be in DC. The first event is right here, in three nights, like you said."

Her lips tightened. "So, I'm convenient. Logistically."

"I prefer to think of it as serendipity."

"Kismet?"

"Exactly!"

She glanced to the side, seemingly unconvinced. "Then there's the fact that you already know the family. Went to school with my sister. And my father likes you. Always has." That last bit was probably the most relevant. The king had practically beamed at him when he'd offered up Sofia's name as a candidate. In fact, hers was the first name that came to him.

She was guileless and genuine, not interested in any kind of career that a relationship with a prince might advance. Having Sofia help with this assured that it would remain confidential.

"Look. I know how preposterous all this must sound at first."

She turned back to him. "I don't think you do, Raul."

"Do you think all those celebrity couples are really legitimately together? The ones who happen to show up at various functions together right around the time one or both of them is releasing a movie or dropping new music tracks?"

She shrugged. "Guess I hadn't really thought about it that way."

"And of course, I'll be paying you handsomely for your time. You said you couldn't afford to hire more help for your shop. I can assist with that. Think of it as a business arrangement. Nothing more."

"Nothing more," she repeated, not meeting his gaze, her eyes focused on the half-eaten empanada on her plate.

"The king and I can rest assured about your discretion. That alone is priceless as far as we're both concerned. You can name your price."

Her eyes lifted back to his face then. "I'm not even sure where I'd start with that. With any of this."

"I don't expect an answer tonight. Think about what you'd like to accomplish with your business. Any other goals you may have. What an offer like this could mean to all of those goals."

He'd struck a chord; he could tell by the expression on her face.

"It would be nice not to have to cut corners for once. And then there's the shelter."

"Shelter?"

"I volunteer my grooming services at a local animal shelter. They're always short on donations."

"Well then. Consider my first act as your fiancé to make a sizable one." He would do so regardless of her answer. But she didn't need to know that at the moment.

"I've always wondered about the journalist dinner. Plus…" She hesitated. As if unsure to share her next thought.

"Plus what?"

"It's nothing, never mind."

The way she poked at her appetizer told him

it most definitely was not nothing. "Tell me," he prodded.

"It's just, there's this certain junior politician my stepfather has been trying to set me up with. In order to secure a business deal he has sway over."

Raul did his best not to react. He hadn't seen this turn in the conversation coming. His security had assured him there was no other man. Something tightened in the center of his chest until he heard her next words.

"I'm absolutely not interested. But Phil has been relentless for me to accept the man's weekly dinner invitations."

"I see."

"If I show up at the dinner with…you, it might finally convince them to give up."

"I see. I'm guessing this politician will be at the dinner."

She nodded without hesitation. "Absolutely. He never misses an opportunity to be seen. In fact…" She trailed off again. Raul could guess what she'd been about to say. No doubt this politician had asked her to attend the very same dinner. Rather strange turn of events.

She rubbed a palm down her face. "What will you do if I say no?"

He released a deep sigh. "I don't really know. There is no one else as backup."

Though he'd dated and been linked to scores of women over the years, the choice to ask Sofia had been a simple one as far as he was concerned. Raul knew he could trust her to be discreet. Sofia's loyalty to Luisa alone was enough to make him comfortable that she would keep the secret. On top of all that, Sofia was simply a decent person, one he could confidently trust to keep her word. No need for the humiliation of asking her to sign nondisclosure documents.

He had no doubt that Sofia would keep the secret forever merely because she'd agreed to do so.

"You have no other options? Really?" The wide-eyed look of surprise she gave him told Raul just how unbelievable she found that to be. The truth was, he hadn't really given anyone else all that much consideration. Plus, he knew his strengths as a negotiator. Knew how convincing he could be. And he didn't sway from a decision once he'd made it.

Was there any other reason you only considered Sofia and no one else?

A subtle voice in his head mocked him with the question. He chose to ignore it.

CHAPTER THREE

"ARE YOU SURE you understood him correctly?" Agnes asked two days later as they boarded the metro train heading to the museum district. She hadn't had an opportunity to talk properly about Raul's ask with Agnes due to a packed schedule at the shop yesterday. Now, on their day off, she couldn't wait to run it all by someone else.

Sofia swiped her card at the kiosk and walked through the turnstile, her friend right behind her. "Trust me, that was my first question."

The part of DC where they were headed would be swarming with tourists this time of day on a weekday morning but Sofia didn't care. She needed to talk to someone about Raul and his "offer." He'd mentioned the importance of discretion. Sofia knew Agnes could be trusted to keep all this to herself. She was one of two people on this planet she considered her best friends. The other one being Luisa.

Sofia released a breath of frustration as their train arrived at the entry point and they boarded.

Luisa.

She was the reason this was all happening. As much as Sofia admired her wild spirit and her utter devotion to living life to the fullest, Luisa really should have practiced just a modicum of discretion regarding her affair. On the contrary, a steady flow of salacious pictures popped up featuring her and her lover whenever Sofia scrolled social media.

It took a while to find two seats together as she was right about the tourist situation. Sofia lowered her voice before speaking again. Not that anyone was really paying attention to them. A family of four with two toddlers in tow took up the row in front of them and the parents were much more concerned about containing the spill of various snacks. Everyone else either had earphones in or was focused fully on their phone screens. Often both.

"Where is this kingdom his family rules, anyway?" Agnes asked. "I don't really follow any royals."

Just the imaginary ones she watched in all those movies.

"In the North Atlantic. About a hundred miles south of Greenland. It's a small island nation that his family has ruled for generations."

"Wow. Just like last weekend's feature film."

Sofia ignored that. "I haven't given him an answer yet." Which was unfair of her, she knew. To Raul's credit, he hadn't tried to strong-arm her in response to her nonanswers when he'd called or texted. Simply told her he'd wait until she knew. But time was running out. The dinner was tomorrow night.

Sofia groaned out loud, resting her head against the glass window.

"You know, I'm not sure why you're so torn about this," Agnes said. "You're being asked to spend time with a real-life flesh-and-blood prince. Any other woman would jump at the chance. I sure would."

"It's not that simple."

"Why not? It's exactly like one of those romantic movies that one channel plays every Saturday evening. You could actually live it. Just think."

Agnes spent the rest of the train ride telling her in detail the fantasy plot of the last such movie she'd watched. Part of Sofia was annoyed about the idle chatter when she had other pressing matters on her mind. While another part was thankful for the relatively mindless distraction until they reached their stop and made their way up the escalator.

The sidewalks were packed. The line to the

Smithsonian National Museum of Natural History was predictably long when they walked by. The usual line of food trucks—everything from ice cream, to taco trucks, to gyros—lined the streets. Luckily, their own destination didn't attract nearly the number of visitors. The United States Botanic Garden was the most soothing place in Washington as far as Sofia was concerned. It always helped to spend time there when she needed to clear her head or think. And she definitely needed a clear head at the moment to think on exactly what answer she was going to give Raul before tomorrow night.

Was Agnes right? Was she overthinking it all? Raul had presented her with a once-in-a-lifetime opportunity with no strings attached. Maybe she'd be a fool to turn it down.

"You know, you'd be a fool to turn him down," Agnes said, echoing her thoughts.

They reached the row of colorful agave plants on the ground floor and sat down on the nearby bench. Already the extra oxygen in the air and the vibrant array of plants helped to soothe her frazzled emotions.

"Although, I do have to admit, it's a rather unusual circumstance you've found yourself in," her friend added.

Sofia snickered. "Not according to the prince. To hear him tell it, such arrangements are commonplace among celebrities and other elites. Us commoners wouldn't know, I guess."

"You would if you watched those Saturday-night movies with me. Did he say why he wants you in particular? This isn't some kind of come-on, is it?"

Sofia squashed the silly reaction that surfaced at Agnes's question. Raul had given absolutely zero indication that his offer had anything to do with any sort of attraction. She had no business feeling any kind of way about that.

"No. He swears it's a simple business arrangement. PR for damage control."

"Huh."

"Basically, I'm in the right place at the right time. The first event is the DC journalists' dinner. And I just happen to be in DC. Plus, there's my connection to Luisa."

Agnes nodded. "Right. You two grew close together at that private boarding school in Massachusetts."

A boarding school she'd only been able to attend because her mother was employed as a dorm mother there. For all of Luisa's faults, she was the only one who bothered to acknowledge her. Sofia had never fit in with the trust fund babies and legacy kids who attended the school.

Her inability to find her standing in such a place had had long-term effects. Sofia had always been leery of meeting new people, dating new men. Always on the outside looking in could make a girl shy and reserved.

Luisa hadn't cared that she was the daughter of a school employee. She'd befriended her anyway.

"I'm convinced Luisa's the only reason I wasn't mercilessly bullied at that school."

"And now her brother is asking for your help to take some heat off of her."

"I suppose that's part of the reason. Though I doubt Luisa much cares what people are saying about her. She never has before."

"I know what I'd say if I was the one he'd asked."

If only Sofia could be as certain. By the time the afternoon rolled around and she made her way to the animal shelter for her weekly volunteer stint, she wasn't any closer to a clear-cut decision.

Raul appeared to be a patient man. But it was only a matter of time before he'd come around and demand her answer.

Sofia looked even more shocked to see him than she had two days ago when he'd shown up at her shop. "Raul? How in the world do you keep popping up?"

Ouch. Not even remotely pleased to see him.

That stung the ego a bit. "I'll have you know, I'm not even here for you."

She tapped a finger against her chin and looked him over. "Right. Why are you here then? Looking to adopt a chihuahua? They have two at the moment. Jazzy and Bob."

"Bob? Someone named their dog Bob?"

"Go figure."

"The poor thing. I might have to adopt him just to be able to change his name."

Sofia shifted her weight to one leg and crossed her arms in front of her chest. "I have a lot to do in there, Raul. At least three nail trims and one surly terrier who needs a flea bath."

"Sounds harrowing."

"It's a full afternoon. If you're not here to see me and you're not here to adopt a pet, why are you here?"

Man, she was so cute when she was annoyed. The ever-present flush to her cheeks grew rosier, her eyes somehow brighter in the afternoon sunlight. Her hair was barely contained in that same topknot from the other day. The worn loose T-shirt she had on over baggy jeans shouldn't have looked enticing in the least. Yet, somehow on her the outfit looked fetchingly sexy. He couldn't even explain it, but she looked just as captivating now as she had the other night at dinner wearing a formfitting wrap dress that hugged her curves in all the right ways.

"You said this place needed financial help. I thought I'd stop by with a donation."

"I don't understand. I thought that was a condition of me agreeing to your terms."

He shrugged. "I figured a charity that caters to animals in need shouldn't be part of any negotiations. Not in any context."

"And you decided you had to come deliver it yourself. In person, is that so?"

"It's a rather high amount. I figured I'd explain personally."

Her features softened before she frowned again a moment later. "Is this some kind of ploy to sway me toward saying yes?"

Raul couldn't resist the urge to tease her. "Depends. Is it working? Are you impressed?" In her defense, maybe there was a germ of truth to that statement. Though he'd intended to donate all along, as soon he'd heard the slight hitch in her voice when she talked about her volunteer work here.

She didn't give him a chance to answer. "Wait, how did you know I'd be here anyway? At this particular shelter." Realization dawned behind her eyes as her jaw fell. "Did you have me investigated?"

"That can't come as a surprise. Any new hire

would require a background check. And it's been a while since we were last in touch. A lot could have changed about you since then."

She practically stomped her foot. "I haven't applied to work for you!" She gave her head a shake. "I'm too tired to deal with this now." She marched around him and strode to the door, then stopped before pulling the door open. "You know, I'd be even more impressed if you gave more than your money."

Raul knew when he was being led into a trap. Everything in her demeanor gave it away. But darned if he wasn't enjoying himself. He'd follow along willingly. "What exactly did you have in mind?"

He found the answer to that soon enough when he found himself holding a wet, shivering chihuahua in a tub of water while Sofia soaped him down. He wasn't going to tell her so, but the little fella was kind of cute. In a tiny mongrel sort of way.

"He's shaking. Is he cold?"

Sofia patted the chihuahua's head. "More likely he's scared," she answered. "Poor little guy." She leaned in close to his tiny whiskered face. "It's okay, handsome boy, you can be brave."

Before Raul knew he'd even intended it, he picked up the dog and nestled him against his chest, bundling him close and wrapping his arms around the small trembling body.

Sofia snapped her head up, looked at him in surprise. "You've soaked the entire front of your shirt. And soaped it no less."

He shrugged. "Maybe being snuggled will calm him a bit."

The corners of her lips lifted ever so slightly. "Maybe."

He couldn't tell if her expression appeared amused or mocking but hoped it was the former. Though that wouldn't be all that much better.

"You're rocking," she said a moment later, her smile growing slightly.

Huh. So he was. Swaying from side to side.

If someone had told him this morning that he'd be holding a seven-pound soaking wet and soapy dog against his chest while he swayed to comfort him, Raul would have asked how much Vesovian wine they'd imbibed. But here he was doing just that very thing.

Sofia stepped closer. "Looks like it worked," she said, scratching below the pup's ear. "He's not shaking anymore."

"Well, look at that."

Sofia stood and flashed him a teasing smile. "Looks like you made a friend, Your Highness. Congratulations."

She was jesting, of course, but he did feel rather celebratory.

* * *

The man had stealth reflexes, but he wasn't quite fast enough. Sofia winced as Ceecee the calico swiped at Raul's arm yet again, this time drawing blood.

Raul swore, but to his credit, he kept his grip on the feline while Sofia clipped her final claw. She had to admit, with Raul's help, she and the other volunteers were going to be done much sooner than usual. Though his right forearm was all the worse for the experience. Ceecee was crankier than usual.

Sofia set the clippers down and reached into her apron pocket for a cat treat.

"I daresay she doesn't deserve that," Raul protested.

"You're right," she agreed. "She's a bad kitty. But she gets it anyway."

She set the cat back in her crate, then went behind the counter against the wall of the room. Grabbing several cotton balls and a bottle of antiseptic, she strode back to where he stood.

The scratch was growing angrier and redder by the second. "This may hurt."

Soaking a cotton ball, she took his hand and dabbed at the scratch.

She hadn't thought this through, had been too lackadaisical about what touching the man might do to her insides. Her stomach turned to mush while a warm sensation meandered along her spine.

Get a grip.

She was simply cleansing a cat scratch, hardly a romantic or seductive act. Though she couldn't deny it felt rather intimate. His skin felt warm against her palm, his aftershave teased her nose.

"Thanks," he said against her ear. Was it her imagination or did his voice sound strained?

Probably because he was bleeding. Nothing to do with her.

"You're welcome. And thank you for helping out."

"It was a pleasure." He cast a glance in Ceecee's direction. "Well, mostly."

"You'll find this hard to believe, but I think she actually likes you," Sofia said, gesturing toward the cat.

"Could have fooled me," Raul countered, mock indignation laced in his voice. He didn't quite hide the smile along his lips.

"She does," Sofia insisted. "Just doesn't want to show it," she added, not entirely sure she was still referring to the cat.

Three hours later they finally toweled out the last of the animals and Sofia tossed him a dry towel to clean up with. Though there was only so much a towel was going to help, between his soaked shirt and his throbbing arm.

Though it all might have been worth it to have Sofia nurse his scratched arm the way she had. The way she'd held his hand, gently brushed her fingers along his skin. He'd been sure he'd stopped breathing for several seconds.

"I'll walk you to your car," he told her, pushing away the silly thought. It made zero sense to feel grateful for a cat's scratch.

"No need. I took the metro."

"Then I'll have the driver take you to your apartment."

"I can manage, Raul. You don't have to go out of your way. Like coming here, for instance."

Raul rammed his fingers through the hair at his crown. As much fun as he had with her, despite the wet and messy—and painful—chores she'd roped him into, he didn't understand her at all. "Why are you so stubborn? About the most basic things. I simply want to see you home."

She slammed her palms on her hips. "Yeah, I'll bet."

"What's that supposed to mean?"

"I'm guessing you also want to press me about whether I'll agree to your scheme or not."

He did his best to scrounge up some patience. He couldn't recall the last time anyone had spoken to him in such a manner. Rather than feeling offended, he wanted to lift her by the waist and shake some sense into her. "Would that be so wrong of me if I did? The dinner is tomorrow."

"Yes!"

Relief soared through his chest thinking she was finally giving him an answer. Until she clarified a moment later. "Yes, it would be wrong of you. Considering how little time you gave me to decide."

His righteousness deflated like a balloon. She had a point. Truth be told, he wasn't expecting such resistance.

"Look, if you're playing hard to get to hold out for more money, I already told you, name your price."

It was the wrong thing to say; he knew it immediately by the fury that blazed behind her eyes.

She poked him in the chest none too gently. He knew his bodyguards were discreetly nearby where they'd parked the car. They had to be seeing this. Apparently, they were smart enough to realize there wasn't any real danger.

Though maybe he shouldn't be so sure.

"Of course I'm not holding out for more money. How can you think that?"

"I'm sorry," he said, fully meaning it. "It was a stupid thing to say."

Her features softened, but only slightly.

The sound of a message rang on his phone and he retrieved it, then swore out loud at what he saw there.

"What is it?" Sofia asked.

He swore yet again, a harsher word this time. "There's speculation that Luisa is expecting her married lover's baby."

"Whoa. That is not a good development, is it."

As far as understatements went, Sofia's words certainly qualified. "Father is going to be livid. I'd better call him. This might be the final straw."

"What does that mean?"

Raul rubbed a palm down his face. "He's threatened more than once to disown her if she didn't reform her ways. If this doesn't do it, I'm not sure what will. Expecting a married man's child."

"That's a rather drastic punishment. Luisa doesn't deserve that, no matter what she's done."

His father would argue that score, no doubt. "I should get back to my hotel and call him right away. If you won't accept a ride from my driver, can I at least call you a taxi or something?"

To Raul's surprise, she merely nodded without a stubborn argument. Then she downright shocked him with the next words out of her mouth.

"I'll do it. I'll pretend to be your fiancée."

* * *

What in the world had she just agreed to?

Sofia slammed her apartment door shut and leaned back against it. Her thoughts were a jumbled mess in her head. Raul had just looked so frustrated, at the end of his rope. Then the thought of her dear friend being shunned by her own father had brought a sting to her eyes. The king couldn't be that cruel, could he? Raul sure seemed to think so. No wonder he'd been so adamant about finding a way to make Luisa's proverbial global spotlight go away as much as possible. Pulling out her phone, she brought up all the relevant sites. Luisa's possible pregnancy was the top story on every single one.

"What have you done, dear friend?"

The screen changed into an icon that belonged to her mother. Sofia released a resigned sigh. She'd avoided her mom's calls for the past several days. Any longer and she ran the risk of Ramona showing up at her door. The last thing she needed. She clicked on the accept-call button.

"Hey Mama."

Her mother's affectionate smile greeted her via video call. "Finally. I've been calling and calling you."

"I'm sorry, I've just been really busy. Haven't gotten a chance to answer or call back."

"I won't keep you then. I just wanted to see

how much you were looking forward to dinner tomorrow night."

How could she know? Sofia had literally just left Raul minutes ago. For a split second, Sofia thought Ramona had somehow heard about Raul's offer. Then clarity hit. Her mother thought she'd accepted the invite from her stepfather's favorite politician. Well, did she have news for Ramona.

"Uh… I am but not in the way you think."

"I don't understand."

"I'm going to the journalist dinner. Just not with Aaron."

Even through the small screen, Sofia could see her mother's face wash with confusion. "Who else could you possibly be going with, dear?"

Sofia suppressed a groan. If Ramona only knew. She was about to explain when an incoming text interrupted the call.

There will be a package arriving at your door within minutes. Just a heads-up. R

Turned out to be more like five seconds. Her doorman rang before she'd had a chance to swipe away the text and return to the call with her mother.

Maybe she was chickening out, but she decided to take the reprieve. "Mama, there's someone at the door. I'll call you in the morning and explain everything."

"But—"

Sofia hated to do it but she cut her off. "In the morning, Mama. I promise. I gotta go."

Frank's call came through automatically. "Uh...there's something here for you."

"Right. A package."

Frank cleared his throat. "That's not the word I would use."

Fifteen minutes later, Sofia had to wonder if there'd been something lost in translation. The "package" Raul had referred to turned out to be three racks of ball gowns, and a selection of high-heeled shoes, delivered by a team of three men.

She sent him a simple text that consisted of one question mark, and soon she had a reply.

Please pick one to wear tomorrow night.

That settled it. She was so in over her head. Here she was assuming she could throw on the simple black dress she kept in her closet for formal occasions.

Reaching for her phone, she clicked on Agnes's contact icon. Her friend answered on the first ring, didn't bother with a hello.

"I've been waiting all day for you to call. What'd you decide?"

"I'll tell you all about it soon enough. Right now you have to come over. I could use some help here."

Agnes didn't bother with a goodbye either. The call simply ended. But Sofia had no doubt her doorman would be letting her up within minutes.

Sure enough, Agnes arrived before Sofia had rifled through fewer than half of the dresses. Each one was more gorgeous than the last.

"How in the world can I possibly choose?"

"Wow," was all Agnes could come with as an answer as she lifted an emerald green gown off the rack and fingered the delicate spaghetti straps. "This one is gorgeous."

"They all are."

"There's only one thing to do," Agnes declared.

"What's that?"

"If it takes all night, you have to try every single one on." She followed the last word with what could only be described as a squeal.

"I'm glad one of us is excited."

Agnes gave her an exasperated look. "How in the world are you not more excited about this? It's like Cinderella going to the ball. Or like—"

"I know, one of those movies on Saturday nights."

"That's right. A straight fairy tale. What's really going on?"

"It's all a little overwhelming, that's all."

Agnes squinted her eyes on her. "It's more than that. It has to be. You're actually scared. I didn't recognize it at first because I've never seen you frightened about anything. Not even when that big police dog growled at us because he didn't want his nails trimmed. What's got you so spooked?"

The question brought to the forefront exactly the emotions she'd been hoping to avoid. Her friend was sharp enough to see it.

"I don't exactly have a lot of experience with men," she hedged.

Agnes shrugged. "So? What experience do you need to play pretend for a while?"

"What if I do something silly?" Like really fall for the man when she was pretending to do so? It would be just like her to do such a thing. After all, she'd had a crush on Raul since developing hormones, for heaven's sake.

"I've only had a handful of dates in college," she continued. "And one not-so-serious relationship that turned out to be a complete waste of time when he realized he still had feelings for his ex."

"That's all past history," Agnes reassured.

She had no idea. Sofia had never felt comfortable in the boarding school, where she was clearly a misfit among the offspring of the top tiers of society. Luisa was the only friend she'd made then. None of the boys deemed her worthy enough to ask out. She'd felt awkward and out of place among the elite. The awkwardness had simply followed her through to college until she'd dropped out, then later into adulthood.

"You're not really committing to him," Agnes added. "You're simply playing a part. Like an actress."

"I suppose that makes sense."

"It sure does. Live a little, try to enjoy yourself."

Easier said than done. The truth was, she *was* scared. Scared of all the ways this whole thing could backfire and leave her with a broken heart. She'd had a crush on Raul Abarra since the day she'd first laid eyes on him. Seeing him again had brought all those feelings of attraction storming back. As far as fantasy men went, Raul fit the bill in every way. She could easily lose her heart to him if she forgot for even a moment that none of this was real.

And she couldn't allow that to happen at all costs. She might never recover.

CHAPTER FOUR

RAUL WAITED IN Sofia's charming sitting room and took in her living space. Long-leafed plants hung from a ceramic pot in each corner and a Turkish rug sat in the center of the hardwood floor. Plush throws were thrown over the back cushions of each of two sofas. An upholstered rocking chair sat between them. A colorful tapestry hung on the wall by the door. The apartment suited her. It was clear she'd taken care to make it a comfortable home space that suited her personality. Funny, he'd grown up in a castle with acres and acres of land surrounding him and a beach he could see from his bedroom window. Yet he was charmed by Sofia's small apartment. It lent a coziness, a homeliness he couldn't say was afforded by any of his own residences.

She appeared out of her room and walked hesitantly to where he sat and Raul did a double take upon seeing her.

There was no doubt about it. He wouldn't be

able to take his eyes off her all night. He didn't find himself speechless often but the sight of Sofia tonight quite literally took his breath away and rendered him wordless. She'd chosen an emerald green silk dress that brought out the green specks in her hazel eyes. It flowed just above her knees, the skirt slightly longer in the back. On her feet were strappy stiletto sandals that showed off her toned, shapely calves. And how often had he even noticed a woman's calves before? Her toenails were painted a shade of green slightly darker than the dress. Her hair flowed in loose, lush curls over her shoulders.

When he finally managed to speak, he could only muster one word: "Wow."

When he'd been led up to her apartment by her doorman, he wasn't quite sure what to expect. She'd exceeded any expectations he may have had. To think, his sister took hours to get ready before any formal events and had a team of professionals whose job it was to make her picture perfect. Sofia had less than a day to prepare and had managed by herself.

"Uh...wow good?"

"Definitely, most certainly good."

"Does this work then?" she asked, doing a mini twirl.

She had no idea just how well it was all working for him. "You look amazing, Sofia. A top contender for the loveliest woman there."

She gasped out a small laugh. "Right. I heard Miss Universe is going to be there. Not to mention the latest film darling and beauty influencer."

"They'll have nothing on you—I'm sure of it."

She stepped closer to him. The smell of her perfume tickled his nose and he wanted nothing more than to lean into her and take a long deep whiff. Her flowery, fresh scent reminded him of the white gardenias his kingdom was known for.

"You don't look so bad yourself."

He mimicked the twirl she'd performed just a moment ago, making sure to exaggerate his movements in such a comical way it elicited a hearty chuckle from her.

"Thanks," she said. "I needed a bit of a laugh."

"Oh?"

She placed a palm on her chest. "I'm a bit nervous. This party isn't typically the type of event that's on my social calendar. Not even close."

"Well, I seem to recall that you had not one but two invites." As self-deprecating as she was, the fact of the matter was that a well-heeled local politician had asked her to accompany him. A real invitation unlike his fake one for the sake of paparazzi.

"Complete fluke of fate, I assure you. And

an invitation that was never entertained could hardly be considered meaningful. I would have never gone with Aaron. No matter how hard my stepfather pressed the issue."

Raul was more pleased by that comment than he had any kind of right to be. This arrangement between them might not be real, but the thought of competing for Sofia's attention with another man left a sour taste on his tongue. If he'd ever had that same reaction about another woman, he couldn't recall.

He held out his arm to her. "Well, madame. Your carriage awaits. Shall we?"

She wrapped her arm in the crook of his elbow. "Yes, let's go. Let's get this over with."

He dramatically clasped his other hand against his chest. "You wound me. Is the thought of an evening spent with me so hard to endure?"

She chuckled again. He was beginning to enjoy hearing the sound of her melodic laughter. Would miss it once all this was over. He would miss *her.*

Whoa. He so couldn't go there.

Still, it was hard not to wish things between them were different. That somehow this pretense was real. That Sofia was indeed his intended princess. That their lives weren't so incompatible.

"Raul?" Sofia's voice pulled him out of his ridiculous reverie. They were from two different realities. When it came time for him to really settle down and get married, it would have to be to someone much more suited for life as a royal. Maybe someone who'd even been born into royalty herself. A few contenders came to mind. No one he particularly felt any sort of affection for or attraction to. But that was a secondary concern. Affection was a luxury for someone like him, bound to the duty and responsibility of a kingdom nation. And what good did genuine emotion do anyway? His own parents had been among the lucky few who'd really felt a real love for each other. Look how that had turned out in the end. Losing that love had left his father a defeated man, nearly crippled with grief after its loss.

Any matrimonial bond in Raul's future would merely be to serve the purpose of providing Vesovia with a ruling family and an eventual heir to keep the royal bloodline going. His future wife would be chosen based on her willingness and ability to serve the kingdom.

As disruptive as this ruse was to Sofia's life, at least it was temporary. He couldn't bear to think of her enduring the endless scrutiny and disruption actually being married to Raul Abarra might bring her.

She deserved better.

No, once all this was over, she could go back to her life, wealthier and better established to reach all her goals. In due time, the world would forget who she was and everyone would leave her alone once more.

He'd make sure of it.

She repeated his name.

He pushed away the thoughts and lowered his gaze to hers. "I'm sorry. I'm just admiring how lovely you look. And wishing I had you all to myself a while longer."

Now, why had he gone and admitted such a thing?

Her gasp of surprise nearly had him admitting even more.

"Um…thank you…?" She said the last two words as a question, confusion etched in her features.

Well, he was feeling a bit confused himself.

A different limo waited on the curb for them, this one white. The same driver stood by the passenger side and immediately opened the door for them as they approached. Raul assisted her into the spacious back seat, then sat across from her. Blue light lit up the interior. A minibar stocked with chilling champagne, sparkling water bottles and various snacks took up a quarter of the space. Soft instrumental music sounded from invisible speakers. She'd never driven in such luxury.

Raul pointed to the champagne. "Can I pour you a glass?"

Sofia immediately shook her head to decline. Her middle quaked with nervousness and excitement. She couldn't risk having her head foggy on top of that. Not that she didn't already feel somewhat heady. The way Raul had looked at her upstairs, the words he'd spoken, the clear desire in his eyes had her tingling inside in a way that had yet to subside. "Maybe just some sparkling water."

"Sure thing." He reached over to the bar, his thigh brushing hers in the process. A bolt of electricity shot through her at the contact. She didn't imagine his slight pause before he moved away. He was just as aware of the current between them. The thought made her heady and apprehensive at the same time. Twisting off the cap, he handed her a sweaty glass bottle. Sofia could only hope he didn't notice her trembling fingers as she reached for it.

No such luck. "Sofia, try to relax," he said. "This will be just a fun dinner that gives us a chance to be seen together to get all the gossip started. You'll be fine—just stick by my side."

If he only knew. Being this close to him in such tight quarters had a good deal to do with her nervousness. "I'll do my best to try," she said, forcing a smile.

"That's all I ask. It's all I will ever ask of you."

Sofia believed him. Raul wasn't a man who said or did anything lightly. Look at all the trouble he was going through to take the heat off his sister and to assuage the king.

Sofia tried to take her mind off her nerves by focusing on the lights of the city as they drove past the National Mall. A sizable crowd strolled the sidewalks given the time of day. Events in DC such as the one they were headed to always drew a secondary crowd in addition to the attendees. Support staff, family members and others. Important people tended to have entourages. Which begged a question.

"Why do you have no one around you?" she asked, striving for some sort of distraction from the churning of emotions in her gut.

If Raul was taken aback by the sudden question, he didn't show it. "What makes you think I don't?"

"I haven't seen anyone."

"Look behind you."

Sofia did as he said. Looking out the rear window, she saw nothing out of the ordinary. Just the usual heavy traffic. "I only see a sedan behind us, with the neon sign of a ride share logo."

"Look two cars behind that one."

Sofia squinted out the window once more. "There's an SUV, with rather tinted windows. They're fairly common in this city, usually following..." It dawned on her then. "Friends of yours?" she asked.

"In a sense. The driver and the passenger are two highly trained bodyguards. They've been with me the whole time."

The revelation truly surprised her. She hadn't noticed them, not even once. "Huh? I didn't realize."

The smile he sent her way held a meaning she didn't fully understand. But that made sense. Being a commoner, it hadn't even occurred to her to look for his bodyguards.

"I also have a staff occupying the suite below mine back at the hotel."

That made sense too. "You must think me so naive." There, she'd finally voiced the thought out loud.

"I think nothing of the kind. I know we exist in two rather different realities.

She knew that of course. Still, hearing the words fall from his lips drove the point home further. What did she have in common with a prince?

What if she couldn't pull this off? Nothing about this made sense. How could Raul possibly think she could play act as a princess-to-be? She had none of the qualifications. She wasn't beautiful. She wasn't elegant. She certainly didn't feel refined.

She bathed and groomed animals all day, for heaven's sake. Hardly a vocation for the likes of a princess.

Well, too late to worry about any of that at the moment. And so much for striving for any sort of calm now. She was going to stick out like a sore thumb tonight. Like Raul said, she lived an entirely different reality than the others at this gala.

"Sofia?" Raul's voice interrupted her panic, concern laced in his voice. "You've gone rather pale. Are you all right?"

She swallowed. "I just want to make sure I say and do the right things."

He leaned over, and placed a warm palm on her knee. "You'll be fine," he told her. She knew the gesture was meant to reassure, but his touch just seemed to make her frazzled nerves all that much more splintered.

He gave her knee a gentle squeeze. "Like I said, just stick by me and follow my lead when it comes to any questions about our relationship."

Oh, God! Her panic upped several points. She hadn't even thought of answering questions. She had no idea what she'd say. "Maybe we should have gone over that. Exactly how are we supposed to have gotten together anyway?"

He shrugged and settled back in his seat. "We just stick as close to the truth as possible."

How in the world was she supposed to do that? The truth was that none of this was real.

"You seem doubtful," Raul said.

"I guess I'm not sure exactly what you mean by that."

"Simple. We say we've known each other for years through my sister. A lingering attraction between the two of us was finally acknowledged and here we are."

Well, when he put it that way…

She supposed that was rather close to the truth. The only problem was, it only held true for one of them.

She'd made a horrible mistake. Sofia's heart pounded in her chest as they pulled up to the venue and a million flashbulbs exploded outside. She couldn't go out there. She couldn't step out of this car and smile at all those cameras pretending to know what she was doing.

She turned to face Raul and tell him exactly that but he gave her such a brilliant, confident smile that the words died on her lips. She really didn't have a choice, did she? If she asked him to turn the car around and go back, she had no doubt he would do so.

"It's just paparazzi," Raul leaned over and said

into her ear. "They only want to snap a few pictures. Which is exactly why we're here."

She swallowed. "Right."

"Ready?"

No. But she nodded despite herself.

He exited the car and the next thing she knew, he was escorting her out of her seat. The moment she stepped outside, she realized how soundproof the car was. A roar of noise greeted her—shouted questions, pleas to face another direction and various other commands she could hardly make out. The flash of lights was nearly blinding now.

"This will just take a second," Raul said loudly over the noise, no chance of anyone else hearing him. Sofia could barely hear the words herself. "Then we'll head inside."

Sofia used his solidness against her side to ground her. She had no idea how she managed it, but she even wrangled a smile onto her lips and angled her face from one side to another.

"That's the way," Raul told her. "You're doing great."

"Not so sure about that." But she was doing better than she might have imagined.

Mercifully, Raul took her by the elbow moments later and escorted her inside, a posse of cameramen followed them for several feet, with

Raul's bodyguards making sure they kept their distance.

They entered the glass doors into a crowded lobby area with high ceilings and marble tile floor. A majestic water fountain sat in the middle. Open doors leading to a vast ballroom with hundreds of round tables sat behind it.

An elegantly dressed woman holding a microphone with a cameraman trailing behind her approached them. Raul lifted his hand almost imperceptibly to one of his guards and the man immediately had her halting in her tracks. "No interviews," he told her. The woman appeared ready to argue but wisely decided against it. With a shrug, she turned on her stiletto heels and scanned the room for another target. But not without one last, lingering look in Raul's direction.

Sofia had to wonder if her look of longing had more to do with the man himself and not so much the desire to score an interview.

Sofia could hardly blame the woman if it was the former. Raul cut a stunning figure of a man in his tuxedo. Tall and imposing, even among all these well-heeled and accomplished men, Raul stood out. A true prince, every inch of the man exuded refinement and nobility. Yet this was the same man who helped her give a terrier a flea bath yesterday. And he hadn't complained or even hinted that such a task was beneath someone of his standing.

He was going to be a tough act to follow once all this was over.

Sofia mentally paused as the thought skittered through her brain. Who was she kidding? She'd been comparing men to Raul for most of her adult life. It was no wonder she'd had no luck with any kind of real relationship. Now she'd managed to place herself in a situation that would only further exacerbate that sorry state of affairs.

"Let's get seated," he told her, placing his palm on her lower back. The now-familiar shudder of desire that ran through her body at his touch unnerved her to say the least.

Once they were at the table, Sofia finally released the hold on her breath. That had to be the hardest part. And it was thankfully over. Now all she had to do was sit through a dinner and the scheduled speeches, making sure to use the right fork. A wave of relief washed over her and the tight knot at the base of her spine began to loosen.

Maybe she could really do this after all.

Her relief was short-lived. The man who immediately approached them upon being seated was the last person Sofia wanted to see at that moment.

"Sofia! I heard you might be here. But I wasn't quite sure I believed it."

Aaron Whitmore strode his way toward them, his usual flashy white grin a bit more forced than usual. The congressman her stepfather had tried tirelessly to set her up with. The grin faltered noticeably when he clearly realized whose arm Sofia had come in on.

"Aaron, how nice to see you," she lied through a fake smile. "Please allow me to introduce you to His Royal Highness, Prince Raul Refik Abarra."

Aaron chuckled nervously. "I believe I'm supposed to bow or something, right?"

Raul thrust out his hand to shake Aaron's. "No need. Bows and curtsies are appropriate for my father. Pleased to meet you."

"Likewise," Aaron said, though he sounded anything but pleased. He turned to face her. "So, you are here after all," he said with a smile too tight to be deemed friendly in any way.

"That's right."

"Can we maybe talk?" he asked her. "Privately?"

The gall this man had. No wonder Phil had homed in on him. They appeared to be all too similar.

Aaron turned back to Raul. "No offense."

Raul ignored him, and leveled his gaze to hers. "Sofia?"

As nervous as she was about answering any questions tonight, she found herself wanting to have this particular conversation. To let Aaron know once and for all that there would be no "getting together" for drinks or dinner or anything else between the two of them. Not anytime soon. Actually, not ever.

She nodded in answer to his unspoken yet clear question. "It's okay."

He waited a beat, not even bothering to deign Aaron with another glance. "I'll find us some cocktails." The look he gave her was clear. He didn't intend to go far. Heaven help her, she might have even read a hint of possessiveness behind his eyes.

CHAPTER FIVE

RAUL COULDN'T RECALL when he'd last felt such a strong desire to grab another man by the collar and haul him outside. If this Aaron person wanted to talk privately, Raul would be happy to oblige in Sofia's stead.

Though it couldn't have been more than five minutes or so, it seemed an eternity passed before the politician finally stood up and left her side. About time.

Raul grabbed two flutes of sparkling champagne from a passing server and went back to the table, retaking his seat next to Sofia and handing her one of the drinks.

"Let me guess, the influential politician who can make your stepfather's dreams come true."

She raised the glass in the air. "You would be correct."

"The nerve of the man," he bit out, resisting the urge to curse.

"He's only partially to blame. My stepfather

had no right to try and use me as a bargaining chip in his scheme to secure a business deal."

"What does your mother have to say about all this?"

A flash of hurt passed over her eyes at his question. "My mother is all too ready to follow Phil's lead. I can't really begrudge her though. She gave up a lot and worked very hard to raise me by herself as a single mother. Now that she finally has someone who loves her and treats her well, I'm afraid she's donned the proverbial rose-colored glasses. She's completely blind to his faults."

Raul didn't voice the thought in his head. Rather than protecting her daughter from being used as bait for a business deal, Sofia's mother had chosen her husband's wants instead. At least that's how things appeared from where Raul stood. But what did he know about having a devoted mother? He'd lost his at the onset of becoming a teen. Some days he had to struggle to remember her exact features.

"I see. Is it done then, do you suppose? Has Aaron finally gotten the message?"

Sofia's lips tightened. "It appears so. And hopefully he'll relay it to Phil."

"I can make sure they both fully understand your position, Sofia. Just say the word."

Sofia's eyes widened. "I don't need you to fight any battles for me, Raul. You don't have to play the concerned protector. It's not like I'm really your fiancée."

Ouch. She had a point, but still.

"I merely meant that I can explain to them that we are an item now." She had no idea how persuasive he could be.

"What makes you think I don't intend to tell my mother the truth about us?"

"Do you?"

She tugged her bottom lip with her teeth. "No. Probably not."

He'd figured as much. Sofia and her mother may have been close once, but he got the distinct feeling the stepfather had driven a wedge between them.

"Do you intend to tell Luisa?" she asked.

He shrugged. "If she asks, I'll tell her the truth. Give her an idea of the trouble she's caused. For all her faults, my sister isn't one to betray my confidence." He swirled the ice in his glass. "However, it's a moot point. Luisa's wholly preoccupied with her affair at the moment. I don't think she would concern herself with the outside world enough to notice. Whereas I'm guessing your mother will have more than a few questions for you after tonight."

Sofia took another sip of her drink. "Let's drop it for now, can we?

Avoidance. For the life of him, Raul would

never understand the inclination of some people to try to sidestep an issue rather than confront it head-on. Hopefully, this little charade of theirs would work to convince her stepfather to let go of his matchmaking. But Sofia had to make him understand, in no uncertain terms, that she simply wouldn't be used as a bargaining chip to further the man's ambitions. If Raul had to guess, he'd venture that Sofia had not been firm enough about the whole thing. Probably out of her respect and devotion to her mother.

"I don't want to talk about Aaron or my stepfather anymore," she added.

Raul didn't miss the omission of her mother in that statement. She really wasn't fully acknowledging Ramona's part in all this.

He wasn't about to press. This wasn't the time. "Can I change the subject by telling you how lovely you look?"

She brightened at that. Ran a palm down her midsection. "I was so torn about which dress to go with."

He raised his glass to her. "You chose well."

"I had help. Agnes came to play Pygmalion to my flower girl." She ducked her head. "I have a confession to make."

"What is it?"

"I have to admit, I had more fun playing dress-up and trying on those gowns than I expected."

"Glad to hear it. When do you think you might wear it again? Or any of the others?"

She set her glass down to give him a quizzical look. "What do you mean? I have no intention of keeping this dress. Let alone all of them."

"Well, I certainly have no use for them. None of them are likely to fit."

His lame attempt at a joke fell flat. Sofia didn't so much as crack a smile. "I can't accept such an extravagant gift."

"You can consider it part of your compensation then."

She shook her head. "Thank you, but no. And it's not like I'll even have a use for such an addition to my wardrobe. As a pet groomer, I don't often find myself attending many galas such as this one. Unlike you, as a royal. You probably have one of these a week."

"You have no idea." Raul tossed back his drink, polishing it off.

"What's that mean?" she asked, merriment swimming behind her eyes.

"It can be a bit much."

"Oh, sure," she said dryly. "How awful it must be going from one grand event to another."

"There's more to it than just attending a party. I have to make sure to say the right things, represent the palace in a fitting way, make sure to play the role of dignitary, representative and royal family member at every moment. Not letting up for so much as a second." The part of being a prince he didn't relish, and would be loath to subject anyone else to who wasn't geared for such an existence from a young age.

"Huh. I never thought of it that way."

"You'd be surprised. It's why I'm looking forward to three weeks from now, when I can finally find some peace."

"What's in three weeks?"

"I'll be heading to Mont-Tremblant, Canada. For some much-needed isolation and peace. No one in that town cares who I am. And I have a place in the mountains. Snow, cold and quiet. The ideal prescription."

It couldn't come a moment too soon. But a nagging thought occurred to him as he studied Sofia. Their little arrangement would be over by then. She'd go back to her life in DC. Suddenly, the isolation and lack of notoriety he so looked forward to in his jaunts to Mont-Tremblant didn't hold the same appeal.

For the first time ever, maybe he didn't want to be alone there.

"How about a nightcap to celebrate the end of a perfect evening?"

Sofia settled in the back seat of the limo and

rested her head against the leather. She knew she should say no, that the best course of action would be to turn down Raul's offer.

But he was right; the dinner had gone off without a hitch, even accounting for the run-in with Aaron. She'd even managed to make small talk with her table mates.

Besides, her phone was still lighting up with messages from both her mom and Phil. The urge to procrastinate returning those calls was tough to ignore.

"Sure, why not?" she answered. Though she was probably going to stick with water or juice. Enough champagne for one night.

"You've earned it. Did you happen to enjoy yourself even a little?"

She was surprised at the answer to that question. Once the food had been served and the lights dimmed, the dinner was in fact rather entertaining. The well-known comedian who'd served as emcee had been amusing and knew how to work an audience. "I did, actually. The speeches were rather funny as was the emcee. Who knew politicians and journalists could be so good at poking fun at themselves and each other."

"The jokes are definitely the highlight of these dinners."

"I thought you said you didn't enjoy these events?"

"I happened to have enjoyed this one. Must have been the company." Something flashed behind Raul's eyes as he said the words. Combined with the deepness of his tone, it sent a wave of warmth over her skin.

She gave herself a mental forehead thwack. He was merely being polite. Why was she looking any further into his words than was warranted? The last event he asked her to attend with him was in two weeks. And he'd revealed this evening that he had a solo trip planned to the Laurentian Mountains outside Montreal immediately afterward. By then, he wouldn't give her another thought. She knew she couldn't say the same about him.

Just. Stop.

That's exactly the kind of thinking she'd been concerned about when she'd hesitated to take him up on the fake-engagement ploy. No feelings could be involved.

A message dinged on his phone and he glanced at the screen. "The hotel has confirmed that the rooftop restaurant will remain open for us and the staff is awaiting our arrival."

"I hope we're not keeping any of the staff over their shift."

He sent her a handsome smile, his features thrown in shadow by the soft interior lights in the vehicle. "It's part of the arrangement when I stay there. At that particular hotel, they're to have the restaurants open with private quarters throughout the duration of my stay. Day or night."

So much of his lifestyle she would never be able to relate to. Not many people could.

Moments later they were at the front entrance of the hotel and two doormen came out to greet them. They rode the elevator to the top floor. Sure enough, a full staff awaited them when they reached the roof, uniformed and all. A minibuffet of snacks and finger foods had been set up in the center. Next to it was a round table laden with pastries and desserts, including an entire layered chocolate cake topped with raspberries. A candlelit table sat in the middle of the area with two chairs and two place settings, next to a standing tray with a bottle of wine. The lights of DC glowed in the distance.

Despite their having eaten, dinner seemed like hours ago. Not to mention, she'd hardly been able to enjoy her meal given the circumstances that had led her there.

Plus, she'd never been good at resisting sweets, particularly when it came to chocolate.

"Will this do?"

He had no idea. With the acting part of the night over, Sofia felt a loosening in the pit of her stomach. She didn't have to pretend right now, didn't have to worry about saying or doing the wrong thing. It was as if Raul had thought of that and made sure the evening ended on a pleasant note. For her.

"This is magnificent. Thank you, Raul."

"My pleasure." He shrugged off his tuxedo jacket and threw it on one of the barstools nearby. Sofia took it as a cue to kick off her high heels. Her calves ached from having them on all night. She didn't even own a pair of high heels and hadn't worn a pair since her high school prom all those years ago.

Raul's bow tie came off next. He proceeded to undo the top few buttons of his shirt, exposing a tanned vee of toned chest, then he rolled up his sleeves to reveal muscled forearms. In a matter of seconds he'd gone from a picture of refined elegance to one of rugged, hardened male. Sofia had to force her gaze away to keep from staring.

"Where shall we start?" he asked, placing his palm on the small of her back in a gesture that was now becoming all too familiar. And all too welcome. He led her toward the food.

Moments later, they were seated at the table. Sofia delved into the cake and helped herself to a forkful, heavy on the frosting. Rich, buttery cocoa flavor exploded on her tongue. She practically groaned out loud with pleasure.

"I take it you like it," Raul said with a chuckle. A goblet of red wine was balanced between his fingers.

"It's like I've stepped into chocolate nirvana."

"I'll have to make a note of it."

"Of what?" Sofia asked, resisting the urge to take another generous bite and talk with her mouth full.

"That you're particularly fond of chocolate."

"That's hardly a secret around these parts."

"Well, if we're going to spend the next couple of weeks together, it will be helpful to know what your likes and dislikes are."

Right. So he could forget about any such facts right after, when it became irrelevant what she preferred for dessert as far as he was concerned.

"That goes both ways," she told him, swallowing another forkful and washing it down with cucumber-mint water. "For instance, I wouldn't have pegged you as a movie fan."

His eyebrows lifted. "What gave you the impression that I am?"

"I just assumed, given that we'll be attending the wedding of an actress. Are you a fan of hers?"

Her tone held a tint of something she couldn't

quite place. She refused to believe it was any kind of jealousy rearing its ugly head.

"Not quite. Going to that wedding has nothing to do with her."

Well, that was rather curious. "Oh?"

"I happen to be well acquainted with the groom, in fact. Rafe and I attended boarding school together in Canada. Much like you and Luisa."

"And just like us, the two of you stayed in touch all these years." She lifted her fork in a mock salute.

"To friends."

Raul raised his glass then chuckled. "Rafe and I didn't exactly start out as friends."

"Really?"

He shook his head, pointing to the small scar along his jawline that had been there since she'd known him. "No, this would be his doing actually."

She hadn't expected that. "You got that scar in a fight?"

"That's right. What would have been your guess?"

She shrugged. "I just assumed you'd taken a fall on one of your many ski trips. Or had some kind of mishap with a fishing pole. You are the outdoor type."

"Nope. It happened because of a wound courtesy of a man I consider a dear friend. In fact, he asked me to be his best man but I turned him down for his own sake. And his bride's."

"You didn't want to overshadow the main event."

He nodded once. "Precisely."

"I had no idea that scar was the result of a fight."

He smiled at her over his wineglass. "You look incredulous. Is it that hard to believe?"

"Well, yes, to be honest."

"Why's that?"

"I didn't expect the only son of the king of Vesovia to get into physical brawls."

"Yeah, well. Neither did my father. Or myself for that matter. Rafe set us both straight on that assumption."

"Just one question then. Did you deserve it?"

He didn't hesitate with his answer. "Oh, most definitely. If anything, he let me off easy. Not that I didn't land a few blows myself. We were both pretty bloody and bruised afterward."

Her jaw went slack with surprise. This was a side of Raul she'd never even considered him having. "What did you do to make him angry?"

Raul rubbed his forehead and ducked his head as if embarrassed. "I'm not proud of my behavior those first few months, after..."

He didn't need to specify. Sofia could guess

he was referring to the period after he'd lost his mother. She knew Luisa had tried to cope by acting out and misbehaving. She still was. But Sofia hadn't considered Raul might have had a reactionary rebellious period of his own.

She remained silent, allowing him to discuss his lost mother further if he so desired. She wasn't going to pry in any way. Judging by what she'd heard and witnessed from Luisa, the queen's sudden death from an undiagnosed blood disorder had shocked and devastated her family.

Several beats passed in silence before Raul spoke again. "I was rather angry at the world back then. And trying to take it out on anyone who crossed my path."

"How so?"

"Ignoring my lessons. Refusing to attend functions." He tapped his scar. "Picking fights."

"People react to grief in different ways." She'd seen it firsthand. Her mother had been a shell of herself the first year after her father had left them.

"Yeah, well, my answer was to infuriate my father and try to provoke classmates. Most of them didn't dare retaliate, too afraid of the ire of the king."

"But not Rafe."

He chuckled. "Nope. Not him. He told me

later he figured it would be worth expulsion to wipe that irritatingly smug look off my face."

Sofia's heart lurched in her chest at the grief-stricken young man he must have been, trying to hide behind a cloak of bravado.

"I wish I could go back and change my behavior. I'll never forgive myself for the way I let my father down. He was already grieving and suffering the loss of his wife. And Luisa and I did nothing but add to his anguish."

Sofia reached out and covered his large hand with her own. "You were both grappling with a pretty big loss yourselves."

"That's no excuse."

She gripped his hand tighter. "I'd beg to argue. It most certainly is."

"It's no wonder he sent us both away to boarding school."

Raul didn't see the discrepancy in his reasoning. As a teen, he'd lost his loving mother. Then he'd been sent away from his very home to deal with his grief on his own. She wasn't finding fault with the king or the way he'd dealt with his own loss, but there was no question he hadn't been able to find it in him to offer comfort his son or daughter.

"I think you're being too hard on yourself. And the vulnerable young man you had been back then."

He didn't respond to that. A curtain seemed to fall behind his eyes and he pulled his hand away. "All I can do is try to make it up to him. And to try and rein in Luisa as best as is humanly possible."

What a load he carried on his shoulders. As if the responsibility of being heir to a kingdom wasn't enough.

What had possessed him to get into all that? He didn't particularly care to talk about his mother or the way he'd behaved after her loss. The aftermath of their lives after she'd gone wasn't a pleasant chapter. Past history that should very well stay in the past. Something about being outside on the roof of the hotel, with the lights of the city bright on the horizon and the warm breeze in the air, it all served to have him loosening his guard and opening up to Sofia in a way he hadn't expected.

Luisa had often said Sofia was the one friend she felt most comfortable confiding in. He'd apparently fallen under the same spell.

"Can I get you anything else, sir?" A waiter had appeared by his side while Raul had been deep in his thoughts. He hadn't even seen the man approach.

"No, thank you," he answered with a look to Sofia first to confirm.

She pushed back from the table as the man began to clear their plates. "I should start making my way back home. I hadn't realized just how late it was. I must apologize to your driver for having to set out this time of night."

Did she really think he had any intention of sending her away? When he had practically a whole floor to himself here at the hotel?

"Well, you wouldn't have to do that if you just stayed here." He held a hand up to ward off the protest that was clearly coming. "I have an entire floor to myself. There's a whole suite that will sit empty. Makes no sense for you to leave at this hour."

She spread her arms, gesturing to her dress. "I have nothing with me. I can hardly sleep in this gown."

"Don't worry about that. It's already been taken care of."

She tilted her head in question. "Taken care of how?"

"Anything you may need has been delivered to my quarters downstairs. You'll find a selection of sleepwear, clothing for the morning, as well as toiletries."

She studied him, her lips pursed. Honestly, what was there to think about? They were pretending to be engaged for all the world to believe. It made no sense for her to be shy about spending the night in the same hotel.

"I guess that's reasonable. I would feel rather bad having your driver leave at this hour and then have to drive back."

He nodded, more than a little relieved that she wasn't going to fight him. She seemed pretty inclined to do so more often than not.

"Wise decision. And this will give us a chance to have breakfast together tomorrow morning and discuss our next steps."

She swallowed. "I suppose we should do that."

"By this time in three days, we'll have touched down in Toronto. The wedding is the day after we land."

Then they'd be onto the next phase. In another country where she'd be traveling with him as his fiancée.

It was well past midnight by the time they entered his suite on the penthouse floor. Sofia appeared dead on her feet.

"Let's get you into bed, shall we?" Sofia's eyes grew wide. The words were out of his mouth before Raul registered how they could be misconstrued. He wasn't actually going to put her to bed himself. As tempting an idea as that was.

He led her to the corner of the room. "That closet is where you'll find the items that have been sent up for you."

"Thanks." Sofia opened the door and stepped inside. "Wow, this is certainly excessive. So many choices."

It so happened one of the choices in sleepwear was a lacy, skimpy number that hung right in the center of the rack. Sofia's gasp of surprise made it clear that she'd seen it just as he had.

Raul couldn't help the images that flooded his head. Sofia lying in bed, in a tangle of silk sheets, wearing the lingerie. The skirt riding up her thighs as she tossed and turned. Heaven help him, the image that followed that scene was her beckoning him to join her on the bed. Pulling her against him, wrapping her arms around his center.

He pushed the picture away and swallowed the curse on the tip of his tongue.

He should have left explicit instructions about exactly what his staff should have provided. He should have asked for thick, baggy flannel pajamas that went all the way down to her ankles. Only, Sofia would most definitely look alluring even in such attire. The thought of her in bed close by was enough to fire his libido.

Not good.

Raul cleared his throat. "I'll leave you to it then," he told her. "You should have everything you need. Good night," he added, then turned to make his way toward his own suite.

"Good night. And thank you," Sofia's soft voice came from behind him.

It was going to be a long night. One thing was for certain: he'd have to take a cold shower before trying to go to sleep. Though he doubted it would help all that much.

That theory proved correct two hours later as he lay in bed staring at the patterned ceiling. Had Sofia chosen that particular nightie to sleep in? Was she sound asleep right now? Was there any chance she might be dreaming of him, the same way he was captivated by her traveling like a temptress through his own thoughts?

He sure wasn't going to get any sleep anytime soon.

This deepening attraction to her was most inconvenient. Sure, they had to be convincing to the rest of the world to present themselves as a couple in love. But any true emotion would only complicate matters. They would be going their separate ways as soon as the ruse was over. It was bad enough he was asking her to take a temporary break from all that she had in her life. She'd left her business to Agnes's care, and she wouldn't see her friends or her home for weeks as she pretended to be something she wasn't.

He had no right to risk asking her for anything more.

* * *

Sofia rubbed a palm over her midriff, smoothing the silky material of the wisp that could hardly be called a nightgown. Why in the world had she chosen to wear this? But after Raul had left the room, she'd found herself lifting the hanger where it hung, removing the thin straps and then putting it on. It so wasn't her usual getup of loose T-shirt and baggy boy shorts. But something about the way Raul had looked at her after he'd seen it in the closet… Her skin felt aflame with the memory of that look right now.

Clearly it was the wrong choice of attire, because sleep still eluded her. Though her insomnia probably had more to do with the way her thoughts kept turning to the man sleeping in the other room. What did he wear to bed? She wasn't sure how she knew, or even if she was right. But something told her Raul wasn't the type to wear much when he slept. Perhaps a pair of comfortable pajama bottoms with nothing on top.

And he probably kept the covers low—he seemed the type to run hot at night—exposing his bare chest.

Her breath hitched and she tossed onto her back. She had to get a grip. Morning would be here before she knew it and she had yet to sleep a wink. Ironic, as this had to be the most comfortable bed she'd ever slept in. Not to mention the most luxurious room. To think, she'd be in such posh surroundings daily for the next three weeks. While she played princess. A princess in love. Though none of it was real. She couldn't risk losing sight of that. Which would be all too easy to do if she kept entertaining thoughts of Raul without a shirt on.

Turned out that was easier said than done. By the time the sun was fully shining outside her window, Sofia had only managed intermittent bouts of restless sleep. Hardly restful but there was no use in trying at this late stage. Besides, she could hear noises outside her door, telling her Raul was up and about.

With a resigned sigh, she got up and reached for the satin robe draped over the edge of the bed. To her dismay, it was much shorter than she'd realized, barely covering the tops of her thighs. Well, there was nothing for it. The robe was the only thing she'd brought into the room with her last night. It matched the nightie, making for an outfit clearly geared more toward a night of romance rather than sleep.

Maybe she could make a beeline to the closet before he caught sight of her.

No such luck. Raul, speaking into his phone, was standing mere feet away from her door when she opened it and stepped outside. She was right. He didn't sleep with any kind of shirt on.

He was bare chested right now, a pair of loose cotton pajama bottoms hanging low on his hips

Speaking of romantic nights.

Just stop.

His eyes landed square on her, then lowered to her bare thighs. Sofia couldn't resist the urge to tug the bottom of the robe lower. But that small action only made things worse. The robe's collar lowered in response to reveal the lace of the nightie at her chest. Raul's eyes flashed back up to her neckline.

Great. Now he knew that she had indeed chosen that particular nightgown to wear to bed.

"Thanks," he said into the phone before clicking off the call and tossing it onto a coffee table nearby. All the while, his eyes never left her. "Good morning. How'd you sleep?"

The words were casual enough, but Sofia could swear she heard a hint of a vibration in his tone.

"Very well, thanks," she lied. Hopefully there were no dark circles under her eyes to give her away.

"I didn't expect you to be up so early," he told her.

That would explain the bare chest.

"Sorry I'm not more…uh…presentable," he added.

She forced a smile. Why was her heart pounding so hard? "I could say the same."

"You look great," he said, then flinched. "I just mean that's a nice color on you. The rose gold suits you."

"Uh…thanks?"

The conversation was becoming more and more awkward. No wonder. She wasn't exactly in the habit of waking up in a luxury hotel suite in the company of a royal prince. Or any man, for that matter. Raul had to sense her lack of experience with such things. He'd probably been seduced and charmed by some of the most beautiful women on the planet. How awkward she must seem in comparison.

For the first time in her life, she had to wonder if she might have tried harder with some of her casual dates. If only to give her some proficiency.

Sofia grasped for something else to say. "Might we get ahold of some coffee?" she asked, just as he spoke too.

"I've taken the liberty of ordering some breakfast for us," he said.

Mercifully, a knock sounded on the door at the next moment.

"There it is now," he said and headed toward the door.

A uniformed waiter rolled in a cart laden

with silver covered dishes and, thank heavens, a large steaming carafe. The welcome scent of rich brewed coffee wafted through the air. Sofia's mouth watered.

"I wasn't sure what you were in the mood for," Raul said once the man had transferred his load onto the table off the kitchen area and lifted the covers. "So I tried for variety."

He certainly had. The table held everything from thick omelets to soft-boiled eggs in standing cups. A tray of various pastries sat in the center. A plate of waffles and pancakes rounded out the offerings. There was no way the two of them could eat so much food.

"I'd say you'd ordered enough for breakfast and lunch."

He smiled. "Once I get to know your preferences better, I'll be sure to only order what I know you like."

That sounded very considerate. So why did the statement send a wave of sadness over her? They were barely more than strangers. An insane part of her wished that somehow their circumstances were different. That they were indeed a real couple on the brink of a new relationship. In that exciting stage of getting to know each other and falling in lo—

She didn't let herself complete the thought.

"Usually just coffee and toast. But this all looks delicious."

"Noted for next time." Without asking, he poured her a cup and handed it to her with a small pitcher of cream.

Maybe he knew a bit about her after all.

Sofia took a deep inhale of the aromatic brew before stirring in a generous drop of cream. She took the seat at the table Raul pulled out for her.

"I was just about to check online," he told her, taking a chair himself across the round table. "To see how much of an impression we made our first night being seen together."

Sofia took as large a gulp of coffee as the beverage's heat would allow and gave herself a second to savor the taste. It was divine. She would guess this particular blend was a bit further on the quality scale than the minicups she used back at home.

He pulled his phone out of his pocket and began to scroll. An expression she couldn't read crossed over his features. "Hmm."

"What is it?"

"There are plenty of pictures of us at the dinner. Along with a good amount of speculation."

"Good. That's good."

"There's more." He stood and walked over to her side of the table and handed her the phone. "See for yourself."

Sofia stared at the screen, expecting to see a picture of the two of them entering the ball-room. But the featured photo of the website wasn't taken at the event at all. No, they'd been snapped sitting head-to-head at the table on the rooftop afterward.

"I don't understand."

"Guess the tabloid sites wanted to go with a more intimate photo."

Suddenly, her appetite was totally gone. Being seen at a dinner was one thing. But the rooftop last night had felt more private. More intimate.

But rather than being bothered, Raul returned to his chair and went about eating his break-fast. He popped a piece of waffle into his mouth around a satisfied smile. In fact, he appeared rather pleased. Which begged the question…

"Wait a minute. Did you have anything to do with this photo?"

He looked up from his cup, his brows fur-rowed. "What do you mean?"

She pointed to the phone screen. "Was this your doing? Is this what last night on the roof was really about?"

He shook his head slowly. "I had nothing to do with it. Though I must say I don't under-stand why you're upset. This is precisely what we wanted. The internet is abuzz with rumors about us."

He was right. He didn't understand at all. She was indeed upset. Because a naive part of her had believed that some of those moments between them on the roof were more than a photo opportunity. That at least some part of last night might have been real.

It had been for her.

CHAPTER SIX

THIS PLANE RIDE was sure to be an uneasy one if Raul couldn't figure out a way to clear the air while they were up here.

Now, studying her across from him staring out the plane window at the clouds outside, Sofia still seemed rather miffed. He really didn't understand why. The entire day yesterday had been strained, the tension between them near tangible. He hadn't been sure what to say to make it better. Then she'd left to go by her shop to ensure everything was in place to have it run smoothly in her absence. He was half-afraid she wouldn't return.

He decided to chalk it up to nerves about leaving her business and home for the next three weeks. Though it sounded like her shop would be in good hands. Her friend Agnes had apparently recruited a cousin to help out along with a few shelter volunteers to round out the staffing needs. Still, the fact that she was leaving her business for so long to assist him served to once again trigger the nagging guilt at what he'd asked of her.

Now, to top it off, something about the photo of the two of them on the rooftop had upset her.

"Sofia."

She turned silently, one eyebrow raised in question.

He cleared his throat. It was tough to find a way to apologize when one wasn't sure exactly what they were to be sorry for. As far as he was concerned, the posting of the unexpected snapshot had only served in their favor. It had driven gossip about Luisa out of the limelight until he and the king could figure out a long-term plan to address his sister's antics.

"I'm sorry if the photo upset you. I can have my staff look into exactly who took it and see they answer for their actions."

Her jaw fell open in surprise. "You think I'm looking to have someone punished?"

"If it will make you feel better."

Now she looked downright aghast. "Why would that make me feel better?"

Raul had to fight the urge to throw his hands in the air. Honestly, what did she want from him? She released a deep sigh and rubbed her forehead.

"Look, I guess I wasn't expecting that I would

be game for that kind of intrusion at any given moment. I wasn't prepared. I will be from now on. Lesson learned."

Raul wanted to kick himself. She was right. He should have prepared her much better. He was so used to consistently and perpetually being under the proverbial microscope, it hadn't even occurred to him that level of exposure might be too much for anyone used to living a normal existence.

As if he needed another reminder that he had no business dragging someone like Sofia into such an existence for longer than absolutely necessary.

"I appreciate that," he told her, though the words were hardly adequate.

She granted him a pensive smile before turning her attention back to the clouds. Hours later, when the familiar sight of the CN Tower appeared on the horizon outside the window, he still couldn't be sure if his apology had been nearly enough.

A sleek town car awaited them when they landed in Toronto. Sofia did her best to take in the sights of the city as they drove but her mind insisted on being preoccupied.

So the second leg of their ruse was now in full live mode. By this time tomorrow night, she'd be getting ready to attend one of the most talked-about weddings of the decade. The wedding of a beautiful award-winning actress to a man who'd gone to boarding school with a prince. A prince who happened to be her date.

A small chuckle of disbelief escaped her lips.

"What's so funny?" Raul asked. He'd done that thing where he'd unbuttoned his shirt collar and rolled up his sleeves again. How did the man look so rugged yet still polished simply by undoing a few buttons?

"I'm just having a hard time believing all this," she admitted. "I guess it's finally sinking in.

As Raul leaned closer, the scent of his after-shave sent a tingling sense of longing through her center. Dangerous combination at the moment—the way he looked and the way he smelled. Given their close proximity to each other in the car, it was wreaking havoc on her faculties.

With everything going on the moment, the last thing she needed was this nonsensical attraction she felt for him to rear itself. But her senses had other ideas.

"I'm sure you'll fit in fine. You might even have fun."

Ha! Easy for him to say. "Not likely. I'll be much too nervous among all those dignitaries, world-famous entertainers and who knows who else way beyond my station."

His mouth quirked into a frown. "There will be no one there above your station, as you call it. As for Rafe and Frannie, they're two of the most down-to-earth people you're likely to meet."

By Frannie, he meant Francesca Tate. Her last movie release had been a blockbuster. As had most of her others. Sofia had never heard her referred to as Frannie before. A nickname reserved for her inner circle, no doubt. A circle Sofia was about to crash under a false pretense.

"They'll love having you at their wedding," Raul reassured her.

He sounded so confident, but Sofia knew better. She supposed most people would seem down-to-earth to a prince in comparison. Even a world-famous Canadian actress and her groom, who happened to be heir to an electronics fortune.

"And the castle is breathtaking. Wait until you see it."

Sofia bit down a gasp. "They're getting married in a castle?"

He nodded. "Casa Loma. It's one of Toronto's most historic sights."

A castle. She really was going in blind here. What exactly did one wear to an actress and tycoon's wedding in a castle?

It was as if Raul read her thoughts. "As with the journalist dinner, you'll have an array of gowns to choose from. And you'll have some more help getting ready for this one, considering it's an affair with much more international attention."

"Help how?"

He narrowed his eyes on her, as if confused by the question. "A team. You'll have a team to assist you."

"A team?"

He nodded. "Yes. A stylist, a hair artist and other professionals to make sure you look the part."

Right. She was playing the part of a princess. A role she had no experience for, despite Raul's reassurances about how well she'd fit in.

Twenty minutes later, the car came to a stop in front of a tall high-rise. A doorman awaited them on the sidewalk just like back in DC. Would she ever get used to someone waiting on the street just to open a car door for her? Sofia doubted it.

"Is this where we're staying while we're in Toronto?" she asked Raul once they reached the marble-tiled lobby.

"Considering I own the penthouse suite, it makes the most sense." He waited until they were alone in the elevator before adding, "You'll have your own room of course."

The elevator doors opened right into his living space. A large foyer with tall green trees along the walls. The entire front wall was glass. The city skyline glittered in the distance outside. "We're by the theater district," Raul told her, leading her inside.

So he owned a cottage in the Laurentian Mountains and a penthouse in one of the country's most metropolitan cities. She recalled Luisa telling her years ago that her brother was more than a prince, that he was a successful businessman who'd grown the family's and the kingdom's wealth by several degrees. Sofia had had no idea of the true extent of his success.

She walked over to look out the glass wall. A whole city lay beneath her, lit up and bustling with nightlife. The theater district. In another reality, she might have enjoyed a romantic night on the town with a handsome date. But she was essentially here to complete a job, to playact a role. Too bad she couldn't ask Francesca Tate for thespian tips.

"Your quarters are to the right," Raul said behind her. "If you'd like to freshen up. I know it was a rather long flight."

She could certainly use the opportunity. Plus, there was another much less pleasant task she still hadn't tackled.

"Thanks. I also need to make a phone call I've been avoiding."

He braced his shoulder on the wall, leaned against it and crossed his arms. "Your mother."

"Correct." And she was most definitely not looking forward to it.

A wave of sadness hit her like a tsunami. Up until a few years ago, she had never kept anything from Mama. Let alone something as major as a fake relationship with a real prince. The idea of lying to her mother seemed so foreign and unnatural.

Yet here she was about to do exactly that. But she had no choice. Not if she wanted to abide by her promise to Raul. Anything she told to Mama, she may as well tell Phil directly. The end result would be the same.

How could one relationship change someone's personality to such a drastic extent? Her mother was no longer her own person; instead she was an extension of Sofia's stepfather now. The two of them were one unit. Which some people might find romantic. Sofia merely found it stifling and hurtful, given that the relationship had come at the cost of her own relationship with Ramona.

"I've been dodging some calls myself," Raul said from across the room.

"I take it you're referring to the king."

He nodded. "You take it right," he answered, a heavy weariness in his voice.

For the first time, it occurred to Sofia just how much of a toll this must be taking on him as well. As busy as he was, with everything on his mind, he had to put on a happy face and present himself to the world as a man who'd recently and unexpectedly fallen in love.

Maybe they were both in over their heads.

The next day went by in a flurry of activity. Sofia had always wondered about the dogs she helped groom at the dog shows. How they managed to sit still for hours as they were prepped and primped before the competition. She figured she had a pretty good idea now.

The fashion stylist had come first to help her pick out a dress and put together the complete outfit. The woman had arrived with an actual wooden chest on wheels full of accessories. She'd left Sofia with three different options of dresses to pick from. Then came the hair stylist. As a result, Sofia was now sporting an elegant updo with tiny sparkles sprinkled throughout her tresses. Finally, a tall, rambunctiously talkative gentleman with braids down to his waist had shown up to do her makeup. He'd used no less than seven different makeup brushes and the process had taken close to an hour.

At least all the preparation helped to take her mind off the phone call with Mama yesterday. To say her mother was surprised about the turn of events regarding Sofia's love life would be a vast understatement. Sofia had no doubt that once it really sank in, her mother and Phil would try to brainstorm any way the new development might help realize her stepfather's objectives. Phil was probably giddy with the idea of a crown prince being someone he might be able to turn to for a favor or two.

Little did he know.

Now, she stood in front of the mirror in yet another silk robe—this one blessedly longer, as it actually reached her knees—to study the end result.

She looked somehow different yet it was still her face staring back at her in the mirror. What would Raul think of the difference? He wasn't here to ask. He'd been gone most of the day, having left early to attend to some business in a local office in the city. She humphed out loud. He probably wouldn't even notice.

The professionals who'd worked on her seemed to think she looked the part. But his was the opinion that mattered, wasn't it? He'd essentially hired her to play the role of his intended princess.

If only Agnes were here. Sofia could use some

feedback from her friend. Not that there was any time to backtrack any of it at this late hour. With a sigh she walked to the closet where the three dresses hung on a hanger.

Time to decide. They were all truly breathtaking. It was so hard to choose. She'd never understood why some celebrities changed into multiple outfits during the same event until now.

Eenie...meenie...

No. That was no way to pick. Funny, she wasn't typically so indecisive. In the end, she went with the first of the three. A midnight blue, tea-length number that the stylist assured complemented her figure and her coloring. Backless, it left her skin exposed down to her waist from behind. A bit more exposed than her usual taste. But these weren't exactly typical circumstances. Sofia disrobed and trailed her fingers down the fabric. As if handling delicate artwork—because in a sense that's what this dress was, a work of art—she slipped it on feet first, taking care not to mar her makeup or dislodge so much as a single hair.

She adjusted the thin spaghetti straps over her shoulders and turned to study the complete look in the mirror.

There. Transformation complete.

Those well-heeled wedding guests would never be able to guess that she made her living elbow deep in soap suds wrangling often filthy pets clean, sometimes while trying to eradicate fleas.

She tried to picture the reaction one of those guests might have if Sofia discussed how she made a living. The idea made her chuckle out loud just as a knock sounded on the door.

Raul's voice echoed from behind the wood. "Is it okay to come in? Are you decent?"

Hopefully, she was a level or two above "decent."

This was the fanciest dress she'd ever worn. The fabric felt like a light cloud over her skin. And certainly no team of professionals had ever tended to her hair or makeup before.

"I can come back later," he said a moment later when she still hadn't answered. Why was she hesitating? This was as ready as she was going to get. Except, maybe she should have gone with the red dress instead.

She could ask Raul. But that idea was nixed in an instant. He had more-important things on his mind. With a steadying breath she went to answer the door and let him in.

She caught him mid-knock. His mouth fell open when he saw her, and his eyes widened. "Wow. That was worth the wait. You look absolutely stunning."

Sofia felt her shoulders sag with relief. She

NINA SINGH   115

wasn't even aware until that moment just how nervous she'd been about Raul's reaction. The man was used to dating international models, prima donnas and beautiful heiresses. A very real part of her worried that she wouldn't measure up as his date to this wedding, no matter how many professionals helped her prepare for it.

"So this will do then?" she asked, hating the doubt that even she heard in her voice.

He swallowed with a nod. "I'd say. Just one problem though."

Her heart sank. She knew it. Something about her was off. "A problem?"

He shook his head, eyed her from the top of her head to the strapped stiletto shoes at her feet. "There's a real risk you might upstage the actual bride."

Ha! Very little chance of that happening. "The day I upstage *the* Francesca Tate will be a day of miracles. At her own wedding, no less."

He leaned a shoulder against the doorframe, and crossed his arms in front of his chest, his gaze level on hers. "I wouldn't be so sure, Sofia. You're a vision in that dress."

She resisted the urge to squeal in delight as she felt warmth flush over her cheeks. Most likely, Raul was simply being charming. Still Sofia felt the compliment clear to her core. She wasn't used to being told she was a vision by the opposite sex, couldn't recall a single time it had happened before. To think, her first real heartfelt compliment from a man came from a crown prince.

A vision.

She could say the same for him. Dressed in a white tuxedo for this event, he looked every inch the prince that he was. Gold cuff links sparkled from his sleeves. His dark hair a striking contrast against the ivory fabric of his jacket. Regal, elegant, polished. And it all came so effortlessly.

He held his arm out to her. "If you're ready, madame, your carriage awaits."

Turned out, Raul had been quite literal with his last comment upstairs.

Instead of the limo she'd been expecting like back in DC, Raul led her out of the lobby and toward a domed wooden carriage complete with gold trim and large round wheels. A waiting driver with a top hat and tailed jacket approached them and helped Sofia up into the seat. He tipped his hat to Raul as he stepped in before going around to the front.

"I figured we'd ride in style. This will take a bit longer to get us there but it will give you a chance to take in the city."

Sofia couldn't help but feel moved by the gesture. She trailed a finger along the beige satin padding of the seat.

"If you'd rather a more conventional ride, we can summon a car instead."

"No, this is perfect. And no horses required."

He flashed her a wide smile. "That's right. It's one of those novel electric carriages. I believe this might be the first one of its kind in the city."

She'd heard about these newer vehicles. Given her love of animals, Raul had made an ideal choice as far as he was concerned. The feeling of warmth in her chest grew.

Careful.

That warm feeling could all too easily ignite into an all-out burn considering how handsome he looked and the way his knee kept brushing against hers in the tight quarters between the plush seats.

She returned his smile with a grin of her own. "I can't imagine a better transport."

Raul leaned over to give the driver the signal that they were ready to go. The man popped open the lid of a center console and pushed a button. A low humming sound echoed from the front and small fairy lights turned on by their feet and through the interior. Though it was still light outside, the lights added to the festive, happy mood.

She focused on her surroundings as the carriage moved into traffic. They'd no doubt draw a good deal of attention but it would be worth it. A nagging voice in her head wondered if the attention was Raul's true intent with the carriage idea. But she would push it aside for now. The CN Tower loomed over the city in the distance.

Raul pointed to it. "You know, you can see that tower no matter where you are in Toronto."

"That's amazing."

"And it rotates, giving observers a full view of the city scape every seventy minutes or so."

A wistful feeling swept over her as she looked at the majestic structure. Too bad they didn't have any plans to visit the landmark. Who knew when she'd ever get a chance to be back in this city. She debated asking whether they had any chance of getting there before leaving for Montreal but Raul answered her unspoken question.

"If we had more time, I would have scheduled a stop for us there. But unfortunately the agenda just doesn't allow it. We have to leave for Montreal in two days and I have another full day of meetings tomorrow. My Canada team is making sure to utilize as much of my attention as they can while I'm here." A clear note of apology interlaced his voice. She wasn't naive enough to think it might be regret.

"I understand," she told him. "It's okay, really. Maybe I'll find a way to get back here with Agnes or something."

Agnes would be the logical choice, though it would be logistically difficult for both of them to leave the shop. Even with the new hires she planned to recruit, they were the most senior and experienced. But Sofia certainly didn't anticipate having a man in her life anytime soon to go traveling with. As far as her mom…well, a few years ago, the first person she would have considered bringing back here was her mother. But Ramona was no longer the devoted, dedicated mom who dropped everything to spend time with her daughter these days. Phil had changed all that when he'd arrived in their lives. Who knew Sofia would find herself missing the borderline smothering parent Ramona had been.

Thank heavens for Agnes. The woman had started out as her part-time employee and developed into a true friend.

"And where did you just travel off to?" Raul asked.

She shrugged her shoulders and allowed herself a smile. "I'm just admiring all the sights."

That was true enough. Around them the city was bustling with activity. Sofia could hardly decide where to look as they made their way through the streets. Tourists with their phones out to snap photos or follow directions. Some who were clear locals with a clear destination in mind. A street performer stood juggling half a dozen long tubes to the delight of the circle of children watching. A long line circled around the sidewalk in front of an elegant building.

Raul followed her gaze to the building. "That's the Princess of Wales Theatre. Not sure what it's showing right now but clearly it's a popular choice.

"Clearly," Sofia agreed.

Several people turned as they passed to watch them go by. More than a few pointed or lifted their phones presumably for a photo.

For the first time since this whole charade started, Sofia actually felt like she might be in a fairy tale starring as the princess. Some kind of Cinderella. She would enjoy it while she could. Because just like Cinderella, all this would end and she would go back to her regular life working long hours grooming during the day and cleaning up at night. Followed by paperwork at home in the evening before falling asleep on her couch from exhaustion.

It was only a matter of time before the clock struck midnight.

CHAPTER SEVEN

RAUL WAS TRYING his best to play the competent tour guide; he really was. But it was so hard to concentrate on anything else with Sofia looking the way she did and with her soft, delicate perfume wafting to him even with the open-air carriage. He'd almost lost the ability to speak entirely when he'd followed her downstairs from the penthouse and seen the low-cut back of her dress. His fingers itched to trail along her neck and down her spine. And lower.

The woman could sure pull off wearing formal gowns. And he'd thought she'd looked good at the gala dinner back in DC. Tonight she looked downright jaw-dropping. He'd only been partially kidding when he'd told her she risked overshadowing the bride. She certainly would in his eyes.

She looked elegant, lovely. Kissable.

Whoa. Steady there, fella.

That was an avenue he couldn't travel down.

So why couldn't he stop thinking about it? He'd hardly concentrated on anything he'd been told during his meetings, his thoughts solely focused on her and where she might be in the process of preparing for the big event. She pulled to him even when they weren't together in the same place. His thoughts drifted to her when he should have been working. Never before had a woman broken into his consciousness as often as Sofia seemed to. For the life of him he couldn't figure out why. Previous time spent with other women had been pleasurable enough. Though he didn't recall ever finding himself fantasizing about those others during his normal routines. And he and Sofia hadn't even been intimate.

Perhaps that was the issue. His imagination was focused on what he knew he couldn't have. Forbidden fruit and all.

Now he couldn't seem to stop himself from wondering what she might taste like if he took those ruby-red lips with his own. How soft she'd feel under his touch.

Maybe they should have taken separate transportation.

But watching her at the moment told him arranging for the carriage had been the right move. As they moved through downtown Toronto, she observed the city with wonder and awe. All the landmarks he himself had grown to take for granted when he visited the city he considered his second home.

"This is fantastic, Raul. Really. Thank you," she told him, her gaze still fixed on her street.

"You're welcome," he replied. She had no idea how selfish his true motives were. Sure, he'd been telling her the truth about wanting her to see the sights of the city as they made their way to Casa Loma for the wedding. But the deeper truth was that he wanted to spend some more time with her, alone, after being away most of the day and before the brouhaha that was sure to commence at the wedding of one of the biggest movie stars in the world.

And besides, she really did seem enthralled by all that she was looking at. "If you do find yourself back in Toronto in the future, I'd be happy to point out some spots you won't want to miss next time."

She turned away from the open window to look at him. "Thanks, Raul. That would be most welcome," she said, her tone pleasant enough. But he hadn't imagined the tightening of her smile as she said the words.

"So, what should I know about these friends of yours?" she asked, jarring him somewhat with the sudden change in topic. "Aside from the fact that one is responsible for a rather angry looking scar on your chin and the other happens to be a major box office draw no matter what genre of movie she's starring in."

"Hmm. That's a fairly accurate description. I can only add that the two fell madly in love with each other and no one saw it coming, particularly the two of them."

She lifted an eyebrow in question. "Oh?"

"Rafe's firm was helping finance one of her movies set in Australia. It most definitely was not love at first sight. In fact, I've never seen Rafe so agitated by a woman before."

"You're kidding? And now they're getting married?"

It still made Raul chuckle when he thought about all the long, drawn-out phone calls he'd get from Rafe complaining about the spoiled, entitled actress who was making his life so irksome. "That's right," he answered. "They would butt heads about almost every decision. Frannie wanted the scenes to look perfect, thought it was worth the cost. Rafe, financier that he is, did analyses and formulas and pushed back whenever he thought things were getting excessive."

"I can see how that might have vexed her."

"They both did a fair amount of vexing, believe me. That's the funny thing."

"What?"

"Throughout my many conversations with Rafe when they first met, I distinctly got the impression that at some point he began to enjoy getting a rise out of her."

Sofia laughed, a soft sound that reminded him of the gentle breeze that rustled the trees back in Vesovia during early-fall mornings. He lost his train of thought before wrangling it back with no small amount of effort.

He continued, "If I had to bet, I'd guess Frannie got her own enjoyment out of the sparring. She likes a challenge and people don't often push back against anything she says or does. I think she found Rafe refreshing for not coddling her like everyone else."

"Sounds like a match made in heaven," Sofia said, her smile still solidly in place. But her eyes were distant and unfocused, and her voice held a hint of melancholy.

He couldn't read too deeply into that.

"Everyone should be so lucky," he said, surprising himself by how much he meant those words. An unfamiliar sensation churned in his gut that he refused to acknowledge as envy. Rafe deserved every bit of happiness in his life and the love of a woman like Frannie. He was honorable, loyal, and had been a good friend throughout the years.

But his friend had never had to worry about the upheaval he would bring upon a woman's life by loving her.

Raul wished he could say the same for himself.

* * *

They were headed to a verifiable castle. Complete with rising towers and a sprawling, colorful garden. Casa Loma was the most magnificent structure Sofia had ever laid eyes on. And that was saying something coming from someone who lived in DC. But while the Capitol Building, White House and One First Street were architectural marvels, Casa Loma looked like something out of a classic fairy tale.

"Your friends seem to have picked quite the setting to get married."

Raul smiled at her. "This is one of only a few standing castles in North America."

"I'd venture to guess it might be the most magnificent one."

It occurred to her then. The man beside her actually made his home in a place like this. Here she was, awestruck at this spectacular specimen of a building while to Raul, it was no different than coming home at the end of the day.

She couldn't let herself linger on that reality for too long or she might very well bid him goodbye and run back toward the theater district on foot.

Soon, they had come to a stop in front of the main door and Raul helped her out of the carriage. If Sofia had thought there'd been a lot of paparazzi at the journalists' dinner, it was scant in comparison to what they came across when they arrived at the wedding venue. There was actually a media helicopter circling in the air above.

The clicking of the numerous cameras as they made their way out of the carriage created a tidal wave of noise. Questions were being shouted at them from every direction.

"Try to relax," Raul whispered in her ear, a charming smile set on his face as he waved to the paparazzi. "We'll be inside in just a moment."

That moment couldn't come soon enough.

"No photographers in there?"

He shook his head. "Just the half a dozen or so professional wedding photographers Rafe and Frannie hired."

Half a dozen? That sounded a tad excessive. But what did she know? She wasn't an accomplished actress about to marry a successful financier. Sofia couldn't imagine the planning that must have gone into a wedding on this scale with the whole world watching.

Rafe pulled her closer to his side as he continued moving forward through the line of onlookers and cameras. So many cameras.

Sofia sucked in a breath of relief when they were finally at the entrance.

"Wow." That was all she could think to say

as she took in her surroundings. The Great Hall was a spectacular sight to behold. A high ceiling that had to be at least sixty feet up. Wooden arches above. An assortment of flags hung from the walls. An indoor balcony with a circular stairway nestled in the far corner.

"Frannie fell in love with this place when she filmed a movie here a few years back," Raul told her. "It's a popular location for films. That movie about the teen wizards was filmed here, for one. As well as the fairy tale with the beastly monster who turns into a prince." He chuckled as he explained.

That's why it looked somewhat familiar.

"It's magnificent. I had no idea there was a medieval castle overlooking Toronto," she admitted.

"Reminds me a bit of Versailles in France."

"Wouldn't know. I've never been there."

"You really must go."

Sofia ignored the sinking feeling in her chest at his words. Raul kept mentioning trips she should take, like back in the carriage when he'd spoken about coming back to Toronto sometime. It never occurred to him to even offer traveling with her. Rather telling, wasn't it?

"If it's anything like this, I would love to see it someday," she said, hearing the wistfulness in her own voice.

"It's much flashier. With more gold."

A smiling woman with a tight bun atop her head wearing a sharp navy blazer and matching skirt approached them. She greeted Raul with a friendly smile. "Welcome, Your Highness," she said before turning to her. "And madame. The ceremony will be held in the Conservatory, if you'll follow me."

She led them down long, narrow corridors, her heels clicking on the hardwood floor. The sound of chatter grew louder as they walked.

"Here we are," the woman said as they entered what appeared to be a man-made indoor Eden. The ceiling above them was a colorful stained-glass dome, the floor shiny patterned tile. Tall rectangular windows behind the podium looked out to a lush green garden.

Suddenly, all the chatter seemed to gradually subside until the room grew completely quiet. She and Raul appeared to be among the last to arrive. Rows and rows of chairs were occupied by sharply dressed, impeccably coiffed guests. Sofia understood why Raul might be one of the handful of people in the world who had to arrive at events after everyone else but she could have done without all the eyes landing on them all at once and watching their every step as their greeter showed them to their seats. Their chairs were in the very first row. An older gentleman nodded his head in Raul's direction as they sat.

Then again, being seen was the point of all this, wasn't it? That was the only reason Sofia was even here to begin with. An organ began to play from behind them, a beautiful, soulful melody that Sofia had never heard before. Six men in dark tuxedos walked in from the back archway, each of them strikingly handsome. They made their way to the front of the room and stood by the podium, turning to face the guests.

The music continued as a beat later six women walked down the center aisle, holding colorful bouquets of flowers in front. Sofia recognized one of them as a talk show host who graced her TV every weekday morning with lifestyle features. She was sure the bridesmaid behind her was a fashion model she'd seen often in various magazine spreads, selling everything from high-end perfume to fashion lingerie. The woman's eyes landed on Raul and lingered just a moment longer than necessary. He tilted his head every so slightly as she passed them by.

Sofia wasn't going to let herself dwell on what any of that might mean.

She sucked in a breath as she recognized the last woman in the procession, a British duchess whose own wedding had just been covered in every major news source.

How in the world was she going to be able to converse with such people when the time came?

She really should have better prepared for this.

As if sensing her tension and panic, Raul reached for her hand next to his thigh and gave it a tight squeeze. Surprisingly, it actually helped. The warmth of his palm sent a calming wave over her skin. Her breath evened to a smoother tempo.

The music faded and then the chords of the familiar "Wedding March" began to play. A tall, elegant man with a boutonniere and a cummerbund that matched the lilac hue of the bridesmaids' dresses entered from the side and made his way to stand in front of the podium, nodding to the bridal party when he got there. The groom.

Sofia wasn't sure what she'd been expecting but if she had to pick what Raul's best friend might have looked like, she wouldn't have been too far off the mark. The two men didn't have much in common physically. Rafe was blond with softer facial features to Raul's tanned skin and dark charcoal hair. But both of them had an aura of authority and confidence that she could sense a mile away. It wasn't hard to see why they'd butted heads in school, then become close friends later. They matched each other's energy.

There was no mistaking when the bride appeared behind them. Her presence was felt before Sofia turned to the doorway. There stood one of her generation's top talents on the elbow of an older gentleman who had eyes the same shade as her famous sky-blue ones. A murmur of oohs and aahs sounded from the seated crowd as the two began to walk down the aisle, and her smile spread from ear to ear as she approached her intended. This was a woman in love. One look at Rafe's grinning face left no doubt that he was floating on a cloud of happiness at the sight of his bride.

A sharp pang jabbed in the vicinity of Sofia's chest. Hard to deny it was anything but envy. She may never have for herself the devotion she was witnessing between these two strangers. No, instead Sofia had to *pretend* she had someone in her life who felt any kind of romantic way about her. For the first time ever, she lamented the lack of a social life. Perhaps she'd given up too soon after all when a date didn't go well. Maybe she should have fought harder for the guy who'd decided to reunite with his ex four months into their courtship.

Instead, she'd been so focused on setting herself up professionally and trying to make sure she was a good daughter to the only parent she had. Look where it had left her ultimately. With no one to come home to at the end of the day and no prospects in sight. Unless one counted the many opportunistic candidates her stepfather kept throwing at her. She felt another supportive squeeze on the hand Raul still held in his. The man was growing much too tuned in to her inner emotions.

Francesca reached her groom's side and they both turned to face the officiator as the music faded to an end. The vows that followed were heartfelt and touching. Sofia might hear the echoes of those words for the rest of her life. In fact, this whole event would be ingrained in her memory for the rest of time. She was in a verifiable castle watching the wedding of the decade on the arm of a prince.

A true fairytale of a day. And just as real.

By the time the officiant spoke the words "You may kiss the bride," the crowd was already on their feet and clapping. Sofia clocked more than one guest dabbing at their eyes with a tissue. Darned if her own weren't stinging ever so slightly.

The now-married couple practically skipped down the aisle afterward, the bridal party trailing after them. The same woman shot another look their way. Sofia cast a side glance in Raul's direction for his reaction. If he noticed the look he'd been cast, he didn't acknowledge it in any way this time. In fact, his gaze was centered solely on *her*.

Sofia didn't imagine the pursing of the bridesmaids' lips as she walked by them.

"Let's get something to eat," Raul said into her ear. "I'm starving. And I'll introduce you to the couple as well as some other guests who should see us together."

Of course. While Sofia was standing here teary-eyed and touched beyond reason at the romantic moment they'd just witnessed, Raul was solely focused on performing for their ruse.

"The dinner is in the library followed by the reception outside," he added.

The other guests seemed to be waiting for the two of them to exit first. Even among this group of VIPs, Raul was given deference. Made sense, the man was a prince after all. He took her by the hand and led her out of the room, nodding to several others in greeting. They walked into a large room with dozens of tables. Glassed cabinets housing hundreds of books served as walls. The bridal party hadn't quite made it to the head table yet, lingering and talking among themselves. The other guests were slowly ambling in behind them. Raul seemed to know where he was going, and Sofia trailed behind him as he walked closer and closer to the head table.

The groom's already-wide grin grew when he

spotted them. He took his new wife by the elbow and led her to where Sofia and Raul stood.

"So it takes nothing less than a wedding to get you to visit," Rafe said when he reached their side. The two men shook hands, then hugged about the shoulders.

Francesca gave her husband a playful punch on the shoulder. "Is that the only reason you married me? To get your friend here to come?"

His answer was a playful kiss on her nose.

Francesca didn't wait for an introduction, turning to her. "So glad to have you here. I'm Francesca."

As if Sofia didn't know exactly who she was. As if most of the world's population didn't know her.

"This is Rafe, my new husband," she added with a brilliant smile.

"I'm Sofia," she answered. "That was a beautiful ceremony."

"She saved her best performance for me," Rafe said on a chuckle, earning him another mock hit.

They were both so utterly charming, their inner light shining so brightly, Sofia felt as if she might be standing in the rays of a brilliant star.

Francesca turned her attention to the prince. "Raul, save a dance for me after dinner. I want to hear all about how you and Sofia got together."

Raul threw his arm over Sofia's shoulder and

pulled her against his side. "It would be my delight, Frannie." The smile he flashed her was several watts strong.

Speaking of charm…he also had charm to spare. The three of them were all accomplished, worldly professionals who were obviously close. As if her feelings of being out of place weren't abundant already. Among them, Sofia felt like a third wheel. Just like she did whenever she was with Phil and her mother.

CHAPTER EIGHT

"Looks like we have prime seating," Sofia said as he led her to their assigned table. It was in the first row in front of where the bridal party sat. "Which makes sense," she continued. "Considering you were supposed to be the best man."

Raul had trouble concentrating on what she was saying. Her dress was the height of distraction. And temptation. The back cut low as it was, he ended up touching her bare skin whenever he reached for her. The way her skin felt under his palm was doing things to his libido he didn't want to acknowledge.

By the time they sat down and dinner was served, he'd had to curl his fingers into his palm.

"This is delicious," Sofia said, around a mouthful of food. "This has to be the most tender salmon I've ever tasted. And the glaze, I think it's pomegranate or something fruity, yet tangy."

She practically moaned in pleasure at the next

bite and the images that flooded his mind had him squeezing his fists tighter to keep from reaching for her again.

She glanced at his plate. "You've barely touched your dinner. Is everything all right?"

Who could eat when he was trying to temper a different kind of appetite? A wholly inappropriate one.

He could hardly tell her the real reason he hadn't taken more than a few bites. "I'm just not thrilled about having to lie to my best friend. At his own wedding."

She set her fork down, and turned her gaze to his. "You mean about us."

He nodded. "That's right. I've never lied to him before."

"I would think you'd be able to trust him with the truth, if it's bothering you that much."

She was right of course. Rafe would keep his confidence if he asked him to.

"I'll tell him eventually. Right now is hardly the right time."

"Of course."

Several people approached their table once the plates were cleared. The curiosity around his mystery date and exactly who Sofia was to him had clearly been causing a lot of chatter throughout the dining room. The interruptions were getting tiresome at this point. Each new introduction irked him all the more. Which made no sense. It was all part of the plan after all.

A woman he recognized as Frannie's assistant approached them and handed Sofia a velvet bag. "Please let me know if the size is accurate."

"What's this?" Sofia asked, taking it from the other woman.

"We give all the women flat, comfortable shoes, miss."

Sofia blinked a question. Raul could tell she wanted badly to ask why she was being gifted footwear but didn't want to appear uninformed.

"Perfect," he said to the assistant. "We plan to do quite a bit of dancing."

The woman tossed a smile his way before making her way to the next table, handing out more shoes.

Sofia pulled out the contents of the bag and gasped in surprise. "These are Italian leather." She trailed a finger over the heel. "Soft as butter."

"I would expect nothing less from Francesca."

"She must really want a full-swing party, with lots of dancing."

He would take that as his cue. Standing from his chair, he held a hand out to her. "Well, we probably shouldn't disappoint her then. Put them on."

She kicked off her high heels and did as he'd asked. "They fit perfectly."

He'd somehow suspected they would. Frannie and her team didn't often make mistakes.

"In that case, please allow me the honor of the first dance."

When they made it outside to the reception party, the night had grown darker, with the sun setting on the horizon. The garden was lit in a cozy blue hue, the Toronto horizon framing the scene. Many of the guests were already there on the dance floor. A mini orchestra played bouncy versions of familiar pop tunes.

Raul took the liberty of removing his tuxedo jacket and tossing it on a nearby chair. He removed his cuff links and rolled up his sleeves.

"Wow. I had no idea you took dancing so seriously."

"Come on. I'll show you just how serious I can be on the dance floor."

She chuckled in response and took his hand. He didn't particularly enjoy dancing. But it surprised him how much he was looking forward to doing so with Sofia.

He gave her a twirl on the way to the dance floor, earning him another laugh. Hearing her laughter never failed to delight him like a toddler receiving a new toy. Melodic and genuine, he imagined the sound of an amused angel might sound similar.

Since when was he so poetic and fanciful

about a woman's laugh? He had to get a grip already.

"Nice footwork," she told him during the first song.

"Several years of regimented dance classes being put to good use."

"Consider me impressed."

"You haven't seen anything yet," he told her, giving her another little twirl.

Essentially flirting with her despite how utterly reckless that was given their circumstances.

How much more of a Cinderella storyline could she be living? Right down to the gifted-shoes plot. Shoes that probably cost more than she might make in a month.

As for her Prince Charming, did the man have to be so good at everything? He was moving around the dance floor like a pro on that competition show she used to watch every season with her mom.

Turned out, now that the party portion of the evening had begun, she was actually enjoying herself. She'd have to be a coma patient not to have fun at such a bash.

And she couldn't ask for a better dance partner. Though he was a rather distracting one. The picture the man made whenever he took his jacket off and rolled up his shirt sleeves would be ingrained in her memory for the rest of time. Sofia couldn't even tell if her breathlessness was caused by all the dancing or the way Raul looked whenever he unbuttoned.

So that settled it. She was going to let go of the last remaining shreds of self-consciousness she'd felt since walking into the castle, stop worrying about how ill at ease and out of place she might feel. She was going to concentrate on enjoying herself. When else would she ever get a chance to dance at a famous actress's wedding reception again in this lifetime?

And the chances of dancing at her own wedding weren't looking very good at the moment. So she would keep dancing until her legs gave out. Or Raul grew tired, whichever came first.

Not that he was showing any hint of slowing down.

As if she'd tempted fate with that last thought, the music suddenly changed. The orchestra didn't stop but rather faded into a different melody. A much slower one.

Fully expecting to stop and walk off the dance floor, she was surprised when Raul held his arms out wide instead. Her breath hitched in her throat. The thought of slow dancing in Raul's arms had blood rushing to her head. She couldn't walk away of course—think of the speculation that might cause. In fact, she'd already hesitated too long. Without giving herself more time to chicken out, she stepped into his embrace and let him sway her in his arms. The now-familiar scent of his aftershave sent a heady wanting through her chest. Being so close against him, feeling his warmth in the cool evening breeze, it was all sending her senses into havoc. She missed a step and he had to grip her tighter to steady her. Heat rushed to her cheeks, leaving no doubt her face was turning red. But she was powerless to stop it. She could just imagine the sight of herself, blushing and breathless in Raul's arms while stumbling over her own feet.

Something else she should have better prepared for: the way she would react when he held her close. So far, she wasn't exactly carrying herself too well. Blessedly, the song finally came to an end. Only the next one wasn't all that much better. A classic love song full of yearning for a new romance.

"I think I could use a refreshment," she said, hearing the breathy sound of her voice.

He hesitated a fraction of a second before letting her go. "I wouldn't mind a drink myself. And maybe a break from dancing for a while."

Rafe gave them a look of question when they passed by him and Francesca on the dance floor. Raul mimicked raising a glass to his lips and Rafe nodded in acknowledgment, though the curious look never left his face. The way he held his new wife so intimately, his hands about her waist, had Sofia blushing harder. She couldn't help but imagine being held that way herself. By Raul.

By the time they reached the bar and secured two sweaty glass bottles of water, she wanted to bypass the drinking part altogether and just pour the contents over her head. Wouldn't that set the tongues wagging with gossip?

"Who? Did you say something?" Raul asked after taking a long swig straight from his bottle.

She hadn't even realized she'd spoken out loud. "I was just thinking how lovely the garden is," she fibbed. "It's an enchanting place for a wedding reception."

He held his hand out to her. "Here, let's take a stroll around. Frannie and Rafe have rented the entire castle. We can take a tour and look around. I know this place has hidden passages."

The thought of being alone in any kind of secret hallway with Raul had her heart nearly jumping out of her chest. The two of them alone in the dark, in the deep recesses of a medieval castle...

Stop right there.

"I'd just as soon avoid those," she told him. "Maybe we could stick to the outdoors. The view is lovely from up here."

"Fair enough."

She took his hand and followed him away from the party. Along the way he reached for his jacket and shrugged it back on. Pity, she rather liked the sight of his strong and tanned forearms. Also, he'd dropped her hand and didn't reach for it again.

The noise of music and partying grew fainter behind them. The night had grown darker with a silver bright full moon casting shadows over the flower beds they passed. They'd walked behind the castle, mostly in silence. Which was fine with Sofia. For the life of her, she couldn't think of a single thing to say.

Her thoughts were a jumbled mess in her head. How could she have been so affected by simply slow dancing with a man? Had Raul felt even remotely the same level of intensity as she had?

She risked a sideways glance at him to see if his face might give her any answers.

No such luck. His profile gave nothing away. If she were a braver, more reckless woman, she might dare to ask. But she wasn't. And there would be no good way to react no matter his answer.

They'd reached a courtyard with a majestic fountain centered between more lush greenery and colorful flowers. Surrounded by immaculately trimmed bushes around the outside, several small fountains spouted water up in the air with a much larger fountain spouting higher in the center. The sound of the water drowned out what remaining noise could be heard from the party on the other side of the castle.

Not for the first time tonight, Sofia felt she might have stepped into some kind of storybook. The beautiful garden, the rushing water. It was a scene out of some romantic movie. And the man beside her perfect in the role of love interest. She studied him now, his hands in his pant pockets, the moon highlighting the dark strands of his hair. More handsome than any man had a right to be. A shiver ran down her spine.

He turned to her. "Cold?" he asked, mistaking her reaction. He shrugged out of his jacket and draped it over her shoulders. The fabric smelled of him and his scent enveloped her. She had to stop herself from leaning into the collar and inhaling deeply.

She couldn't very well admit the real reason for her shaking.

"Do you regret turning down Rafe's request to be a groomsman tonight?" she asked, just to start some sort of conversation.

He shrugged. "If I was anyone else, I would have gladly done it. It wouldn't have been fair to take the spotlight off the wedding couple."

She'd had no idea she was going to ask the

question until the words left her mouth. "Which bridesmaid do you think you'd have been paired with?" She had a feeling she could guess who the lucky lady might have been. The woman who'd sent him the smoldering look as she'd made her way down the aisle during the wedding.

He sighed and raked his fingers through his hair. "It so happens that I do happen to have a bit of a history with one of them."

Hah! She knew it!

"The model. Right?"

His eyes narrowed on her. "How did you know that? We thought we kept it rather discreet."

"Is there…anything between you now then? Still, I mean?" Why in the world was she even going down this path? It really was none of her business.

Raul stepped closer to her. "Why are you asking me that, Sofia?"

Something snapped within and she didn't have the heart to lie in answer. She'd opened herself up with her question and didn't see a way to back out now. Nor did she even think she wanted to.

"Can you not guess why?"

His eyes darkened and a muscle twitched along his jaw. "I don't want to misunderstand in any way. Help me understand."

Sofia swallowed. Was he really going to make

her come out and say it? She wasn't sure how she might even find the words.

She took a breath and began to try. "I saw the way she was looking at you. Possessive. Familiar."

"And?" he prompted.

"And it made me feel a certain way."

"What kind of way?"

"Jealous," she blurted out before she could stop herself. There. She'd said it. The world seemed to stop for a moment. As if they were suspended in time. The one word hung in the air between them with no way to take it back. "I was jealous that she might have a history with you. I can't really explain why. Just that—"

He didn't let her finish the sentence. Before she could so much as register what was happening, he'd reached her and then his lips were on hers, kissing her. Heat exploded inside her belly and moved lower.

She lost track of time when he finally pulled away. Her limbs trembled with desire and disappointment. Why had he stopped and how could she get him to start once again? Right this second.

"Don't look now, but we happen to have an audience," he whispered against her mouth. "I don't know why, but Frannie's publicist just walked into the courtyard."

Sofia's blood froze in her veins. Was that why he had kissed her? To display their fake relationship to a publicist? It was just a little too perfect, too convenient.

Here she was admitting her attraction, lowering the guard on her heart. Only to wonder if it had played right into some kind of performance. The very possibility squeezed her heart in her chest. How naive of her. How careless. She'd blame the magic of this courtyard for messing with her head. The romantic atmosphere framed by the fountain and the beauty of the flowers surrounding it. All of it had made her forget why she was really here. With a crown prince she barely knew.

She stepped back away from him and shrugged off his jacket, then handed it back to him, making sure to keep her distance.

"Thanks. I'm not cold anymore." Which was a complete lie. In fact, her skin felt completely frosted, as did the area around her heart.

"We should get back," she said, doing her best to steady her voice though it wasn't easy. "You promised Francesca a dance."

Raul watched her walk away, his tuxedo jacket still draped in his hand. He would follow her back to the party of course. He just needed a minute. Maybe several minutes. The kiss had been on an impulse, one he'd been helpless to curtail. Now, he felt as if the world had somehow shifted. His insides felt like mush, his vision was blurry.

After a simple kiss. Such dangerous and treacherous territory.

In a clumsy effort to take it all back, he'd focused on the random excuse that Frannie's publicist was the real motivation behind his actions. To try to convince Sofia the kiss wasn't real. Seeing the woman approach, he'd taken it as a sign. Maybe he'd been callous. He would have to find a way to make that up to her.

But it was better than leading Sofia down any kind of false road.

CHAPTER NINE

Three days later

HE SHOULD NEVER have kissed her. The situation between them was complicated enough without blurring lines unnecessarily. And that earth-shattering kiss had definitely blurred more than a few.

Raul reread the email he'd been trying to focus on for the past ten minutes. His concentration was shot. Sofia had kept her distance since the wedding. Or, to be more accurate, since their kiss.

So she was clearly harboring some regret as well.

He wanted to kick himself. How could he have lost control that way? He had no excuse, really. No matter that Sofia had been a tempting vision in that dress that showed off all her curves. Or the way she'd felt in his arms dancing slowly, the scent of her rose perfume numbing his faculties. Or the way she'd admitted feeling jealous. About him.

He'd simply let it all snap the tight string on his control. The better approach would have been to downplay her admission. Give her a chance to back out of saying such a thing. Instead, he'd let her words go to his head and he'd given in to the relentless desires he'd been fighting for so long. So very wrong of him to toy with her emotions that way. Or his own for that matter. No good could come of any confusion, on either of their parts.

It couldn't happen again; he had to keep his distance. They still had this trip in Montreal to get through while pretending to be engaged.

He reached into the drawer of his desk and pulled out the velvet box. The original plan had been to give it to her on the jet on the way over here from Toronto but Sofia seemed much too tired and distracted. Just as well. This way, when he gave it to her, he could emphasize how much of a prop the ring was. He would tell her that they had to make sure she had it on her finger before their dinner with the mayor tomorrow night. To reiterate that the plan to convince the world they were a couple would be well on its way to completion by then.

His phone rang in his pocket, pulling him out of his reverie. His father.

"Your Highness." Raul said, clicking on the phone.

In his usual customary way, the king didn't bother with pleasantries before getting to the point. "I'm calling to say well done, son."

Raul knew immediately what he was referring to. He and Sofia were featured on a slew of gossip sites. Several photos of the two of them at the wedding were posted on all the apps that mattered. Even the one from the rooftop in DC had resurfaced.

It may have been random, but Frannie's publicists stumbling upon them during such an unguarded moment had sent the gossip mills turning at breakneck speed.

"Thank you, sir. I'm glad it's working."

"Most definitely is," the king replied with enthusiasm. "This is the first morning I haven't heard a thing about Luisa. Every outlet that reports on us is solely focused on you and that lovely young lady you recruited."

Raul cringed inwardly at the last word. Accurate as it was, the term had an uneasy twist curling in his stomach.

"You make sure to keep it up."

"Will do, sir. In fact, the next announcement you'll see is the news that we're engaged to be married."

"Excellent. I'm glad the young lady has been

so agreeable and has played her part so very well." Raul could picture the smile of satisfaction on his father's face.

"Her name is Sofia, Your Highness."

"Yes. Sofia. Please give her my thanks."

"I'll be sure to do that. Any word from Luisa?"

His father grunted in disgust. "Not a one. She isn't answering calls from anyone. Not even me. Just depleting her accounts from various parts of the world as she carries on this ridiculous affair with the man she's fallen for."

For the life of him, Raul couldn't figure out what had gotten into his sister. She'd always been a free spirit, but ignoring the king's calls was akin to self-sabotage.

"Let me know if you hear from her yourself," the king said. "Who knows, maybe all this attention you and the young lady are receiving will bring Luisa up to the surface."

"Sofia," Raul reminded him but the king had already hung up.

Owner of said name was sprawled on the couch scrolling through a tablet screen when Raul left his study after the phone call.

"Are you reading all the salacious gossip that's being written about us?" he asked.

Sofia glanced up in surprise, as if she hadn't heard him approach. "Oh, heavens no. I looked at a few photos and their captions but they were making me much too anxious."

Huh. Most of the women he knew would be grateful for such attention. Maybe Sofia hadn't been the best choice for this endeavor. She'd been uncomfortable with the scrutiny on her from the very beginning.

Not that there was much he could do about the decision now.

"All the chatter has gotten the shop some added business. There's that. Agnes said a couple of outlets called her for information about me but there really isn't much to tell." She sighed.

He leaned to look at the screen over her shoulder. "What's got you so engrossed then?"

She shifted to give him a better view of the tablet. "I'm looking at all the great attractions Montreal has to offer. What a metropolitan city."

He read her latest page. "Montreal Botanical Garden."

She nodded with clear enthusiasm. "The pictures are lovely. The DC botanical museum is one of my favorite places on earth. But it's mostly indoors." She pointed to the screen. "This place looks much larger, sprawling over acres and acres."

"Would you like to go?"

The tablet dropped to her lap. He had her full attention now. "Really?"

He shrugged. "If you want to see it, then we should plan on a visit."

Her mouth fell open before her lips curved into a wide smile. "We? You mean you'd be willing to come along?"

"Of course."

In fact, he couldn't think of a better way to spend the afternoon. They could both use a bit of a reprieve after the excitement of the wedding, then all that had followed after. Fresh air and a long walk among beautiful gardens might be just the thing to restore some of the friendly camaraderie between them that had been sorely lacking since that night at the rooftop in DC. And the kiss hadn't exactly helped.

"I have a meeting downtown followed by a few phone calls back here, but we can leave right after I'm done."

"I can hardly wait," she told him, her smile confirming her words.

The wedding seemed forever ago. Almost as if Sofia had attended it in another lifetime. Her mind registered the event as a distant memory. Except for one part.

The kiss.

That particular moment was seared in her mind as clear as the sky outside their floor-to-ceiling glass window at the luxury hotel they'd be staying in while here in Montreal. Sofia couldn't seem to stop thinking about it. The way Raul's lips had felt on hers. The taste of him. The warmth of his body as he held her tight with that magnificent fountain behind them.

Enough. Raul had only been after a publicity shot. She had to get it through her head that the kiss had meant nothing.

Not to him anyway. How foolish of her to think otherwise for even a moment.

For the umpteenth time this morning, she tried to push the images out of her head as she made her way to her private bathroom. This time last week, she wouldn't have even known that hotel lodgings could be this large and luxurious. Then again, she'd never had occasion to stay in one with an actual prince before. They were in the royal suite of the most exclusive hotel on the Golden Square Mile. Fully stocked kitchen, glass ceiling in the sitting room and not one but two massive terraces overlooking one of the most dynamic parts of the city.

She might miss the shower the most when they had to leave Montreal. Raul sure knew where to stay when he traveled.

Not that she'd seen much of him since they'd arrived. He was either out and about on what he called palace business or at the other end of the suite when he was here.

No doubt to try to avoid her. She could hardly blame him. Things had been strained between them since the night of the wedding. Their conversations had been brief and awkward. Maybe spending time in a beautiful botanical garden would clear the air between them once and for all. And then they could pretend that kiss had never happened. As if.

She should never have done it. Should have never revealed her heart that way and admitted to feeling jealous about a bridesmaid glancing his way. She cringed at the thought now, like she'd been cringing since that night.

Turning on the waterfall shower head, she flipped the switch for the chromotherapy light. The stall was immediately bathed in a soft purple hue. Sofia had never heard of chromotherapy and wasn't sure about the science behind the idea. But there was no denying the sensation of calm that washed over her along with the warm water once she stepped under the spray.

If only the feeling lasted longer than the time it took her to towel off. The problem was, any sense of calm and peace seemed to evaporate as soon as she found herself in Raul's presence. Maybe longer showers were the answer. Maybe she should stay under the water all day, until her skin pruned and her legs grew tired. Then she could just go to bed. That way she could avoid Raul altogether.

Slight problem with that approach, as tempting as it was. They were due to have dinner with the mayor tomorrow night. She probably shouldn't appear wrinkled and waterlogged for it. Oh, and she'd also asked to spend the day with Raul at the Montreal Botanical Garden. Careful what you wish for.

As much as she was looking forward to seeing the famous attraction—considered one of the finest plant and flower museums in the world—she wasn't sure how she might deal with the proverbial elephant in the room.

They couldn't avoid acknowledging what had happened between them much longer.

Could they?

Sofia sighed and turned the knob on the marble-tiled wall, getting the water as hot as she could stand. Finally, when her muscles began to feel like molten lava, she shut the spray and toweled off.

A few minutes later, she was dressed and her hair dried. Raul was waiting for her when she left her suite of rooms. She startled when she saw him, as was usually the case these days.

"Sorry," he apologized. "Didn't mean to surprise you."

"I just didn't realize you were back."

He simply nodded, his gaze bouncing around

her face. "I just have to take a conference call in a few minutes. After that we can head to the gardens."

"I'm ready whenever you are."

He nodded in a jerky motion. If she didn't know him any better, she might even say he was acting nervous.

"Just one thing first," he said, reaching into his pocket and pulling out a small item. Sofia's breath caught when she realized what it was.

"A ring," she said, surprised her mouth was working enough to get even those two simple words out.

"I figure it's time we signified to the world that the relationship is indeed serious."

Sofia had to clamp her lips from laughing hysterically at the statement. Either that or she was going to cry. Their fictitious relationship had to seem serious. So Raul was going to have her wear a ring.

He reached it out to her in the palm of his hand. Pathetic really. The first time in her life she'd be wearing an engagement ring and the man wouldn't even be slipping it on her finger. Because it meant nothing.

"Did you want to…?"

She sucked in a deep breath and lifted it out of his palm. Now that she was really looking at it, it struck her just how beautiful a specimen it was. A large square-cut diamond on a platinum band with smaller rubies on either side. It was stunning. Exactly the kind of ring she may have picked for herself.

"Where did you get this?"

He ducked his head, almost imperceptibly. "I had it ordered back when we were in Toronto. I thought it might suit you."

Sofia couldn't read too much into that statement or his intentions. The fact that he'd actually thought about what kind of ring she might like and had it ordered meant nothing. Simply another part of the act. He wasn't even going to put it on her himself, for heaven's sake.

"It's breathtaking."

His gaze was steady on her now, looking at her expectedly. What else was she supposed to say? Was one supposed to thank a guy for getting a real custom-made, clearly expensive piece of jewelry when the sentiment behind it was completely fake?

"It should fit," he said. "I asked the stylist about the jewelry you had on that night."

So that's what he was waiting for. To make sure he got her finger size right. Sofia grasped the most precious jewelry she'd ever laid her hands on and slipped it on the ring finger of her left hand.

Fighting a silly urge to cry as she did so.

* * *

She had to get some air.

Sofia watched as Raul shut the door of the room he'd been using as his office since they'd arrived to take his phone call. The ring felt heavy on her hand. A heaviness also hung around the vicinity of her chest. Making her way to the terrace that faced the Montreal skyline, she resisted the urge to glance at her ring finger yet again. It was all too easy to stare at the sparkling diamond and red rubies around it.

A cacophony of sounds echoed through the air once she stepped outside. The Golden Square Mile was rich with shops and cafés and all the trappings of a hopping metropolitan city. Another place she'd like to revisit someday under more normal circumstances. She huffed a chuckle at that. She didn't even know what was normal anymore. Kicking off her shoes, she dropped into the nearest lounge chair and stared at the tall buildings that surrounded the hotel.

She didn't know how long she sat there, simply staring at the sky and trying to process exactly what was happening. Finally, when her mind was a jumble of confusing thoughts, she pulled her phone out and clicked on Agnes's contact.

Her friend answered on the first ring. "I've been waiting with bated breath for you to call."

"I know. I've been meaning to. It's just that so much has been happening. And we're barely halfway through with…" She couldn't even come up with an adequate word. "You know."

"Tell me everything," Agnes demanded, a clear tinge of excitement in her voice. "Where are you right at this moment?"

"In the most deluxe suite of the most deluxe hotel I'll probably ever find myself in. I'm currently laying in a lounge chair on a terrace, one of two available to me at that, staring at the tallest of Montreal's buildings with a wall behind me that's covered in shrubbery and flowers."

Agnes let out a whistle as her response.

Sofia continued, "Before that, I took a shower in a marbled bathroom bathed in purple chromotherapy light."

"That sounds like heaven."

"It does, doesn't it?"

Agnes paused a beat before speaking. "So why don't you sound more like someone who's been to nirvana?"

Sofia moved the phone away from her mouth and sighed loudly. "I don't know. It's just so surreal."

"What do you mean?"

"I'm not a real princess candidate. The engagement isn't real even if the ring is."

"Whoa, whoa. Back up. Ring?"

Sofia lifted her left hand and stared at the finger sporting said ring. It was getting much too easy to keep looking at it, and her finger had become much too familiar with the added weight.

"Raul got a ring for me to wear to make this all seem more authentic."

"I bet it's gorgeous. And costs a fortune. Which leads me back to my earlier question. Why do you sound less than thrilled? Are you sad you may have to give it back someday?"

That most certainly wasn't it. Raul wasn't the type to take jewelry back no matter the circumstances. She'd insist of course. There was no reason for her to keep such a costly item.

"You know me better than that."

"You're right. So tell me why."

"I just didn't ever expect that I'd be wearing a fake engagement ring. Not that it's fake. Though he certainly could have spared the expense and gotten costume jewelry. The diamond is real enough." Sofia stopped. Now she was just rambling.

"Why don't you just try and enjoy yourself, Sof? Take the opportunity for what it is. A chance to live an alternate life for a while."

Everything Agnes said made sense of course. So why couldn't Sofia simply flip a switch and enter enjoyment mode? Why did her heart feel so heavy?

The kiss.

It had just complicated everything. Darned if she knew what to do about it.

"That makes sense. There's just a part of me that wishes things were different." That somehow this was all real.

Agnes stayed quiet for so long that Sofia glanced at the screen to make sure they hadn't lost the connection. "Oh. My. God," she finally said several moments later. "You're falling for him, aren't you?"

Oh, no. Was it that obvious in her voice?

"I mean, I can hardly blame you," Agnes added. Her friend's tone grew softer when she spoke again and sounded much more serious. "But I don't want you walking away from all this with a broken heart, Sof."

Sofia didn't say out loud the words that popped into her head. It might already be too late for that. "Don't worry about me, Agnes." She summoned the most reassuring voice she could, then added, "It's probably just a crush. The man is a handsome, successful prince. And we're pretending to be in love. I've simply gotten carried away on occasion. I'll make sure not to let it happen again."

"If you're sure."

"I am. Don't worry," she repeated, hating that she'd managed to make her friend concerned about her. That's when she noticed Raul standing by the door. A brick landed in her stomach. How thick was that glass? The thought that he might have heard any of that mortified her.

"Agnes, I have to go. Will call you later, promise." She clicked off the call without waiting for a response.

There was no telling by the expression on his face how much he may have heard, if anything. Closed book, as always. He tapped twice on the glass door before sliding it open. "Ready to go?"

She forced a smile, hoping she looked as enthusiastic as she'd been feeling this morning when looking at pictures of the gardens online. Had that really just been less than three hours ago?

"As ready as I'll ever be."

CHAPTER TEN

HE'D HANDLED THE whole ring-giving terribly.

Raul replayed the earlier scene in his head and wanted to kick himself. He'd simply wanted to give it to her without any kind of presentation. That's why he had taken the ring out of its original package. Handing Sofia an engagement ring housed in a velvet box would have made the gesture all too real. But in his attempt to make it all seem like a casual necessity that was really no big deal, he'd practically thrown the thing at her and waited until she'd put it on. As if things between them hadn't been awkward already.

All because of that damned kiss.

In hindsight, he probably should have told Sofia about his intentions when he ordered the ring to begin with. Part of him had been uncertain though about whether he would go through with it. Also, it chagrined him to acknowledge that another part of him might have actually wanted to surprise her with it. To pretend for even a moment that he was really about to propose to her, that she was really about to become his future wife. But that idea was preposterous and wholly inappropriate.

Instead, he'd just bungled the whole encounter.

He'd almost backed out of this trip to the botanical garden afterward. For a while right after he'd hung up with Vesovia's chief economist, he'd had every intention of sending Sofia off with his bodyguards to visit the gardens without him. Instead, he'd decided to face his folly and try to smooth things over. Again.

He so missed the easy camaraderie they'd had together when they'd first embarked on this trip.

To her credit, Sofia seemed to have moved on from the whole ordeal. Sitting next to him in the passenger seat of the hired sedan that was taking them out of the Golden Square Mile and toward the outskirts of the city, she enthusiastically watched the scenery outside her window and asked numerous questions about what she saw.

He'd never had such a fun travel companion, despite how unusual the circumstances were. In fact, now that they were on their way to the attraction, Raul couldn't deny feeling a rush of excitement about the outing. When was the last time he'd looked forward to a day spent essentially staring at flowers and shrubs? He couldn't recall.

Maybe that was Sofia's enthusiasm reaching him through proximity.

When they approached the front entrance and he helped her out of the car, that enthusiasm showed through in spades. Her mouth fell open as they strolled down the brick pathway to the fountain in front of the redbrick sprawling central building.

Her eyes widened when they reached the entryway and she stared at the gardens that lined the path.

"I had no idea tulips came in so many colors," she said, her voice dripping with wonder. "There must be thousands of them."

"That's just the start," he told her, draping his arm over her shoulders. A gesture he hadn't even known he'd intended. He'd never been one for outward displays of any kind of affection. Much like his father. And absolutely nothing like his very gregarious sister.

He could just picture his bodyguards smirking in surprise several feet behind them.

As casually as he could, he dropped his arm back down to his side.

"Which garden would you like to go to first?" he asked her. "There are seven of them."

She clasped her hands together in front of her

chest. "I'm way too hyped to decide anything. You pick."

"You might regret that when I tell you my first choice."

She actually did a little circle twirl, her arms outstretched. "How would I possibly regret seeing anything here? Go ahead and pick."

"All right. But no take-backs."

She shook her head in mock solemness and held up a hand. "I hereby swear."

"It's settled then. Let's go."

They passed by the first garden, the Roseraie, with its majestic statue of the cast-iron lion guarding its entrance. Sofia's steps slowed and she cast her eyes about with clear hesitation. "Already regretting your offer? That didn't take long."

"Absolutely not," she answered a little too quickly, hardly sounding convinced. She looked so darned cute when she was fibbing. In fact, she looked more than cute. In a bright blue dress the color of the sky above, with another pair of strapped sandals adorning her feet, she made him yearn to do more than just throw an arm around her shoulder again. Much more. Right here in public.

"Just promise me we'll come back to see all this after wherever it is we're headed."

"Of course we will. We have all day."

Her smile widened. "We do? But you're usually so busy."

"I made sure to clear my schedule."

The area around her eyes softened, and it sent a surge of pleasure through his core. The urge to take her in his arms and kiss her senseless was nearly overwhelming.

"Thank you for doing that," she said softly.

The truth was, he should have been the one thanking her. He was actually taking a day off and enjoying himself, allowing himself to forget all the responsibility that always awaited him. At least for a little while. Instead of telling her any of that, he waved her forward to follow him.

"Come on. If we're lucky we might actually be able to see a butterfly emerging from its chrysalis.

"The insectarium, huh?" That was the first spot in the botanical garden Raul led her to. The large dome structure had displays of various insect species including several breeds of butterflies.

"Isn't it great?" Raul asked. His tone and demeanor at the moment reminded her of a little boy who'd been gifted a highly desired toy. This was a side of him she hadn't seen before. Dressed casually in khaki shorts and a silky soft short-sleeved V-neck that showed off those muscular, distracting arms. To top it off, he sported dark aviator glasses and a deep maroon baseball cap that covered his dark hair.

They'd never actually been out in public before. So this must be what he wore to disguise himself as best he could. So far, it seemed to be working. No one yet had bothered to give them a second glance.

His attire and overall look was no doubt meant to be casual, ordinary. But someone like Raul would never pull off looking anything resembling standard. Casting a quick glance at him now, she had to look away to keep from staring. Even dressed like a tourist, he was stunningly handsome.

She hadn't witnessed him having quite such fun before either. Not even at Francesca Tate's wedding. To think, all it took was thirteen displays of insects and several hundred butterflies flittering about the air from tree to tree in a domed enclosure.

After they'd taken their time going from display to display and then waiting in vain for a chrysalis emergence that unfortunately never occurred, Raul finally indicated he was ready to see the rest of the gardens.

"Okay, your turn," he said once they'd left the dome. "Where would you like to head next?"

Sofia didn't have to think twice. The picture of the beautiful rosebushes had been embedded in her mind since they'd passed them by an hour ago.

As if he could read her mind, Raul said, "Let me guess. Should we head back to the cast-iron lion statue where the rose beds are?"

"You read me so well," Sofia said. Huh, when had that come to pass anyway? Every meal they had together, each dish he'd suggested, had tasted divine. He'd ordered a ring that suited her taste to a tee. She glanced at her hand. It hadn't taken her long to get used to wearing it. Would probably take much longer to get accustomed to being without it when the time came.

"And where did you just drift off to?" he asked. Sofia dropped her hand and shifted her gaze. If only he could guess.

They'd reached the concrete path leading back to where they'd begun. "I was just thinking how the photos I saw online of the Jardin botanique didn't nearly do this place justice."

She could spend days and days here going from one garden display to another. The day had grown brighter when they made their way back to the lion statue.

"If I had to guess what heaven looks like, I'd say at least part of it would include rosebushes just like these."

"And a dome filled with butterflies." he added with a mischievous smile.

"If you say so." Sofia walked over to the nearest rosebush. The flowers were a gorgeous color somewhere between orange and yellow. "I've never seen roses this shade." She leaned to inhale their sweet scent.

They moved onto a bed of pinkish roses that smelled just as lovely yet somehow different.

"I didn't realize roses didn't all smell the same."

"They do to me."

She chuckled at his disaffected tone. "You haven't even tried to smell them. Here, give them a whiff." She gently nudged him forward toward the rosebush.

He did as she asked and when he straightened again, he tilted his head toward her. "These actually remind me of the flowers native to Vesovia that bloom every spring. And also the scent you wear."

Sofia blinked at his words. He'd noticed her perfume and associated her scent with flowers native to his kingdom. She wasn't sure what to do with that kind of information. She decided to move them along.

"How about the Japanese garden next?"

He didn't say anything for a pause, his expression impossible to read behind those dark lenses of his glasses. Something told her it was just as well she couldn't see behind his eyes. Just the way he was standing close to her, his breath rapid, it was all making her pulse skip.

Finally, just when she thought she wasn't going to be able to resist reaching for him, tracing her fingers along his lips, he spoke. "Lead the way."

Right. As if she could get her bearings at the moment to figure out where to go. "I believe it's to the left," he said, somehow sensing her quandary.

"Yes. Let's go then."

Yet neither one of them moved. Silly really. The man had rendered her near dizzy with just a few simple words telling her she smelled like wild roses he associated with his home.

With no small amount of effort, she tore her gaze away from his lips and made her feet move. She tried to make small talk as they found their way out of the rose garden and walked farther along the path. But by the time they'd reached the pathway leading to the Japanese pavilion, she'd run out of ways to say how much she loved the various flowers they passed along their stroll.

They reached a lush green area with a small stream dotted with purple-and-white trees that resembled weeping willow but in color. The sign next to it said Zen Garden. Without asking, Sofia walked over to a bench on the edge of the grass.

"I could use a few moments of Zen if you don't mind."

He smiled, taking a seat next to her. "I don't mind at all, Sofia."

Peaceful.

Raul took a deep breath and just let himself be. Whoever had designed this display sure knew what they were doing. For a rare moment in time, he wasn't running through a list of to-dos in his head. Or thinking about his next conversation with the king about Vesovia's financial outlook. Or about his sister.

The soothing sound of the running stream, the fresh air, the gentle breeze rustling the colorful leaves of the trees all served to relax him in a way he wasn't accustomed to. But those things were only part of the reasons for his current tranquil mood. The woman next to him had a lot to do with it too. Being with her somehow helped to soothe his mind and soul.

Except when he was racked with the desire to kiss her. Like he almost had back in the rose garden. Luckily, he'd come to his senses before he could reach for her and put his lips on hers.

To think he'd been trying so hard and doing so well at keeping his distance since they'd arrived in Montreal. Only to almost lose control and give in to temptation within moments of being alone with her. And out in public no less.

He had to be careful, couldn't let his attraction to her become a distraction. But that was becoming harder and harder to do with each passing day. Sofia's mere presence had added a layer to his life since she'd entered it. A layer he hadn't even known was missing.

When they'd first arrived at the Jardin, she'd actually asked him what he wanted to do first. The simple question had touched him more than he would have guessed. Despite the myriad of decisions he had to make in any given day, he wasn't often given a choice about what he wanted. No, he was more usually acting at the whim of a meticulously planned schedule or along with the demands of the king.

Being asked about his preferences was a new experience altogether.

"So, you like bugs, huh?" she asked now, a teasing quality in her voice. "Guess I learned something about you today. A couple things actually."

He gave a small laugh. No point in mentioning that one of his earliest memories involved running around the palace grounds barefoot, with his mother laughing behind him as he chased a dragonfly. The way she indulged his fascination with the strange-looking fly that he was convinced he could catch if he tried hard enough. He pushed the memory aside.

"And I learned that you really enjoy frolicking in a garden." He refrained from telling her how adorable she looked doing so. Like a cute little sprite dancing about from one bloom to another. "What's the second thing?"

"That you're pretty good at playing regular tourist guy. When you want to."

Her words were meant in jest but the underlying truth in them couldn't be denied. He was, in fact, simply playing at being some kind of regular tourist here today. His reality was much different. A factor he seemed to be forgetting all too often.

Sofia had just given him a needed reminder.

"I have to say," she began. "As much as I love most animals, I'd just as soon stay away from the insect types." She gave an exaggerated shudder.

"Admit it. You enjoyed watching the butterflies flit about at least a little."

She shrugged. "Yes, I will acknowledge that I liked that part." She raised her hand and pinched her thumb and forefinger. "But only a little. As lovely as most butterflies are, if you look too closely at them, you can still see a little insect body." Another shudder.

"Maybe that's the problem. You shouldn't be

looking too closely." There was a metaphor in there somewhere, he was sure.

"Maybe," she acknowledged.

"Though I suppose you're right. Even butterflies aren't as cute as say Sir Bunbun."

That earned him a hearty laugh. "No, I suppose not."

"You really handled it well when he misbehaved. As you did the mix terrier at the shelter. Not to mention the tabby that kept trying to extract a piece of flesh with his sharp claws."

"Thanks, I've had lots of practice wrangling uncooperative pets."

"Have you always been good with animals?" he asked, genuinely curious and somewhat chagrined that he didn't know the answer and hadn't thought to ask before this.

A smile blossomed on her face. "For as long as I can remember, I've preferred their company to most humans."

"I can certainly understand that. Guess you're in the right line of work then."

"Opening the groom shop used up all my savings. I scrounged and worked double shifts at a café for years."

A sense of guilt washed over him. They hadn't seen each other in years and Raul didn't know Sofia as anything more than his sister's friend until just a couple of weeks ago. But if he'd known about her plight, he wouldn't have hesitated to help her. He would have had to up the amount they'd agreed to when she'd accepted playing the role of his fake fiancée. Probably would have done so anyway. She'd certainly earned it.

"It was the next-best thing," she said.

"Next-best thing to what?"

She let out a small laugh. "Silly really. But when I was younger, there was nothing I wanted to do more than study to become a vet. That way I could really help animals."

"Why didn't you?" He had no doubt she would have made a great doctor for animals.

She shrugged as her smile faded. "I began the process. Looked into schools. Applied for loans. It just wasn't meant to be." Her voice had shifted lower, deep with regret.

"What happened?"

"There was never enough money. And then my mom got sick and I helped as she got better. Any extra money went to medical bills. By then I was exhausted and damned near penniless."

Luisa had never said anything about Sofia's mom getting sick. Then again, she didn't often come up as a topic of conversation.

He was really beginning to wish that wasn't the case.

CHAPTER ELEVEN

SOFIA WAS GETTING perilously close to feeling sorry for herself. It was time to move on. Both from this conversation and from the Zen garden, which was apparently relaxing enough to loosen her tongue. She hadn't talked about her thwarted dream of becoming a veterinarian since as long as she could remember. Wasn't sure why she'd even brought it up just now. She'd just been so touched and surprised that Raul actually remembered the name of the dog she'd been tending to when he'd first entered her shop. She gave a shake of her head. There she went, overplaying things again. Sir Bunbun was an unusual name. Of course he would remember.

She clapped her hands on her knees. "I think I'm ready to move on to the bonsai display."

Raul stood without hesitation and they made their way to an enclosed courtyard about an acre away. Inside was an array of small trees sprouting the characteristic branches of bonsai. Surprisingly, there were some as tall as five or six feet. Others were barely more than a few inches, displayed on stone platforms. There had to be close to a hundred trees in this one garden, making for a breathtaking scenery of lush green.

"I had no idea they could grow so big," she said, wandering to one of the taller ones.

"I've seen some even taller. In Japan."

She was going to sound like a broken record if she mentioned wanting to go there to see for herself. It seemed her newly formed list of places she wanted to visit was growing longer and longer by the day.

"That's where this one is from," came a voice behind them. A medium height gentleman wearing thick glasses and holding a pair of specialty scissors walked to where they stood. He had on a chest tag that read Phillipe Franc with the word *curator* underneath. "This is a red pine from the Atami area. I was just about to trim it."

Sofia watched in fascination as the curator began gently pruning a branch. After several moments, he turned to them with a smile. "That should do her for a few months. If you ever get a chance, you should make a trip to one of the many castles in Kyoto. The most spectacular bonsai trees," he told them before wandering off.

"He's right. The castles themselves are sights to behold."

"Trust me," Sofia said, wandering farther down the line of trees. "I'm making a mental list of all the places I've been intrigued by since we started on this little adventure together."

A silly part of her willed him to say the words she knew he never would. That he would be happy to accompany her if she ever had the opportunity to take such trips. But he'd had numerous opportunities to do so, and never even hinted at the possibility.

What did she expect? He had responsibilities. A whole kingdom to help run. One day, he'd be running it himself entirely. Raul didn't have time to gallivant around the world. Let alone with her.

And some day, probably in the not-too-distant future, he'd be planning a honeymoon with his real fiancée. A fiancée who would match his worldliness and regality. Unlike her.

A pang struck through her core and Agnes's voice echoed in her head.

You're falling for him, aren't you?

Heaven help her, she was. With no clue as to how to stop it. But she had to figure it out. Or her heart may never recover if she fell too far.

They left the enclosure and walked farther down the path along the Japanese garden.

Two hours later after they'd meandered through the aquatic garden with its myriad of pools, Sofia realized she was parched. And starving.

Raul's next words yet again had her wondering if he could somehow read her mind. Or maybe he was growing more and more able to tune in to her moods at any given moment the more time they spent together.

What that possibility may imply was too scary to contemplate given how she was supposed to be fighting falling for him and all.

"Think it might be time for a drink and something to eat, if you're agreeable to the idea."

Her stomach answered for her with an audible rumble. How ladylike. And so not future-princess-like in any way.

"The garden has a pretty impressive outdoor restaurant," he said after a small laugh.

"Let's go."

They crossed a bridge overlooking a koi pond. Across the water, a stone lantern sat among the shrubs. Sofia watched as a group of people walked onto the field from the other side. A bridal party. The bride and groom held hands with a trail of sharply dressed people following behind them. She could make out two sets of parents, a little girl carrying a bouquet and another young woman who looked like a sibling to one of the couple. A middle-aged man with a camera rounded out the small group.

He took several pictures of the couple alone. Then the others joined in.

The bride and groom appeared so happy. Couldn't seem to stop touching each other. One of the parents picked up the little girl and pointed to the trees. More photos were taken.

A coil of longing rolled through Sofia's stomach. Francesca and Rafe's wedding had been a doozy of a soirée. And she'd loved being a guest at such a momentous event. Yet this small group of people celebrating love in such a cozy and comfortable way tugged at her, making her yearn for the slim possibility she might have such an experience herself someday.

Then her traitorous mind made things even worse by picturing just such a scene with her in the starring role of new bride. And the man standing by her side happened to be none other than Prince Raul Abarra.

She tore her gaze away from the picture-perfect scene. "I think I could use that drink now."

It wasn't lost on Raul the look on Sofia's face as the bridal party took pictures across from them while they stood on the koi pond bridge. Nor did he fail to notice how quickly she wanted to leave the Japanese garden just then.

Now, as they walked back through the aquatic garden down the pathway, she seemed content to remain silent while admiring the several pools surrounded by colorful native lilies. The garden was less crowded than she would have anticipated and they had no trouble finding a free table.

A server showed up right away to place sweaty bottles of water in front of them and to take their order.

"I would like whatever drink is considered the most popular here," Sofia said. "And the tropical salad."

Raul asked for authentic Canadian ale and the sandwich special. Plus an order of fries with gravy for them to share.

"So tell me what your favorite garden has been so far," he asked after their waiter walked away.

Sofia rubbed her chin. "It would be impossible for me to choose just one. It would be like having to pick from chocolate, ice cream or key lime pie."

He made a mental note to make sure all those items would be stocked in the fridge wherever they stayed from now on. "You're right. Why choose if you don't have to?"

She did a finger-gun motion. "Precisely. I'd say that's a good approach to life in general."

"I can't argue with that."

Their server was back in no time with his ale and he placed a fiery red drink in front Sofia.

He took a sip of his beverage just as he realized what she'd inadvertently ordered. "Sofia, don't—" But he was too late. She took a rather large gulp before sputtering out and clasping the cloth napkin to her mouth.

"Oh, my Ga—" More sputtering followed a large swig of her water. Raul was trying his best not to laugh but it was so very difficult. Her cheeks were turning that charming shade of blush again, her eyes watering. She gulped some more water.

"What is that?" she demanded to know, giving the offending beverage an evil-eye glare.

"Sorry, I realized too late to warn you."

"Warn me how? I thought it was a strawberry daiquiri or something."

"More like a Bloody Mary. But with clam juice and a heavy dose of peppery spice. It's considered a specialty drink around these parts."

Her lips curled. "Clam juice? Pepper?"

"In tangy tomato juice. It's called the Caesar."

"That fits. Because I feel about as betrayed as he was by our waiter. And he seemed so nice."

Raul laughed so loud, one of his bodyguards a couple tables over threw him a curious look. "In his defense, you did ask for the most popular drink here."

"I'll try to be much more specific next time."

He leaned over and pulled the offending drink

away from her toward the side of the tale. "We'll swap it out for something fruitier."

She shook her head. "No way. I'm not taking any more chances," she said lifting the water bottle up and mimicking a toast. "I'll stick to water. Cheers."

She was turning a light shade of green. Her eyes still watering. The napkin dabbing away at her mouth. Yet she still managed to look alluringly sexy. How did the woman possibly pull that off?

There it was, the ever-present desire to take her lips with his own. And more where that came from. He'd been with more than his share of women throughout his adult life. Many of them beautiful seductresses who knew their way around pleasing a man. Yet, he couldn't recall being quite so aroused simply sitting with a woman while they had lunch.

The waiter was back with their food. "Was there something wrong with your drink, madame? I made it myself."

Rather than admonish the man for "betraying" her as she'd described, Sofia gave him a sweet smile and actually apologized. "Sorry, it just wasn't what I was expecting so I'll need to sip a bit slow. It's really quite good."

Huh. Imagine trying to spare the feelings of a stranger over something as innocuous as a drink.

The man smiled with pleasure and left after depositing their food.

"No *'et tu Brute'* then?"

Sofia dabbed at her salad with her fork. "As you said, it was my fault for not checking before ordering. And he said he made it himself."

Raul was beginning to understand why Luisa had found such a lifelong friend in the woman sitting with him. Though the two had nothing in common.

Actually, he was beginning to understand his sister much better these days. Being tempted by forbidden fruit was not an easy struggle. Though Luisa really should have drawn the line at involvement with a married man.

"My mom would actually like that," she said, pointing her fork at the Caesar.

Her mom. He hadn't wanted to ask earlier. Figured Sofia would tell him more if she wanted to talk about it. But curiosity got the better of him. "How is your mother now? You mentioned she was sick for a while?" he asked, hoping he wasn't opening a can of worms.

She smiled with relief. "Thank heavens she's recovered fully." She set down her fork. "Physically anyway."

What a curious statement. "Oh?"

Sofia fingered the rim of her plate and stared across the patio. "She was just different afterward. Not the same woman I grew up with. She was more reckless. More forgiving of men when they didn't treat her right."

Her eyes got a faraway look as she continued to stare at nothing. "I don't think she would have married a man like Phil before the illness."

"People change once life throws them a curve," he said, understanding better than she might have guessed. "Look at Luisa. You met her after her transformation into a wild, unmanageable teenager. As a child, she was always the respectful, well-mannered one of us. While I was the one being chastised by most everyone employed at the palace for one transgression or another."

She turned back to him, an indulgent smile on her face. "I find that hard to believe."

"It's true. My father changed as well after the loss of my mother."

The words were out of his mouth before he even knew he'd intended to say them.

Sofia reached over the table to take Raul's hand in hers. The tone of his voice sounded heavy with painful memories.

"How did the king change?"

He shrugged. "He became distant. A shell of his former self. Refused to acknowledge Luisa's cries for attention until they became extensive.

Sent us both away to boarding schools instead. Then he started putting off major decisions about the castle and kingdom to the point where the staff and national councilors started coming to me instead for guidance and instruction. I wasn't even in my midtwenties yet."

Sofia could just guess the effect all that had on the man sitting before her. He'd been barely more than a teen, dealing with the loss of a parent. On top of the pain, he'd been saddled with responsibilities he was much too young and probably unprepared for.

He pulled his hand out of hers, took off his glasses and pinched the bridge of his nose. The cap came off next. Sunlight glittered in his dark hair; the hat had barely made a dent in his thick curls.

"What about you?"

"What do you mean?"

"You must have changed yourself. You'd just lost your mom."

His lips curled into a smile but it was less than convincing. "I believe I already explained how Rafe and I came to be friends. I was disruptive and incendiary. Picked a fight with anyone who crossed my path."

"You also said that was short-lived. And caused by surface anger that you eventually tackled." And what a strong young man he must have been to have done so. He clearly had no idea how resilient he'd been in the face of such turmoil. "What happened on a deeper level, Raul?"

"I don't think I know what you mean," he said, reaching for his sandwich and taking a bite then chewing quickly. Sofia had to wonder if he even tasted the food he swallowed much too fast.

"There's something I want you to know." Raul's eyes hardened as he spoke. "Luisa never told me about your mom's illness."

He was changing the subject. Clearly he regretted the vulnerable moment just now. Sofia would go along. He wasn't ready to talk any further about the loving mother he lost. Or how the tragedy had upended the life of everyone he loved.

He continued, "She also never told me that you were struggling financially. I would have found a way to make things easier on you."

Maybe he didn't know his sister as well as he thought he did. "You hardly knew me."

"Still."

She shrugged. "Thank you. But your sister offered to help us herself."

He nodded slowly. "I should have known. You turned her down, didn't you? Prideful to a fault."

"I managed to cover what we owed for my mother's medical care."

"What about tuition so you could pursue veterinary school?"

"Luisa offered that as well. But that was much too generous. There was no way I was going to accept."

Besides, what if she'd taken the money then failed her classes? She would have been humiliated to have done so on a friend's dime. With no real source of income to pay the money back.

Raul was right about her pride in that sense.

Sofia knew she didn't want to be beholden to a friend in order to pursue a career. But not for the first time, the question that was always at the edge of her mind popped to the surface once again.

What would have happened with her life if her mother had never gotten sick?

She was still pondering the question hours later when they arrived back at the hotel. Raul had been reserved on the return drive, the conversation between them sparse.

"I have some emails to catch up on," he told her. "Maybe I'll see you later if you're still up. Help yourself to anything in the fridge or feel free to order room service."

He didn't wait for a response before turning on his heel and entering his set of rooms.

Sleep would be futile for a while tonight; her emotions were too raw. She hadn't meant for their conversation back at the garden restaurant to turn so heavy. It seemed as if all the weighted talk had sapped both of their spirits. The hour was still relatively early though. Grabbing a magazine she knew wasn't going to hold her interest, she made her way back to the terrace and lay on her favorite lounge chair, studying the night sky.

She wasn't sure how much time had passed when she was jolted awake, surprised that she'd actually drifted off after all.

Must have been all the fresh air and walking. Plus, deep conversations with a guarded prince could sure tire a girl.

Her phone was alight with missed messages on the cushion by her thigh. She scrolled the screen to find no less than three calls from her mom and half a dozen texts. They all said variations of the same thing.

What in the world is going on?

Engaged, Sofia? please answer your phone!

I'm your mother, tell me what's happening with you!

That last one was followed by several images. Her and Raul, sitting at the garden. In one photo they were smiling at each other across the table; in another they were laughing over the wrongly ordered drink. In yet another she was holding his hand on the table. A gasp sounded from her throat. That last one had zeroed in on her finger, clearly portraying her new engagement ring.

A cold wave washed over her as she processed the images. That's why he'd taken his glasses and hat off then. The whole day was nothing but a photo op. How could she have been so clueless? Just like back in DC atop the hotel after the journalists' dinner. Or when Francesca's publicist had walked in on them at the fountain. Raul wanted nothing more from their time spent together than to have his picture taken with her.

With trembling fingers she began typing out a response

I'm sorry for the shock. Things aren't always as they seem. Will explain later I promise. Please be patient though I know it's hard.

She hit Send and tossed the phone across the chair. Sheer luck kept it from bouncing onto the ground. Silently cursing Phil, she stood and began to pace. If it wasn't for her stepfather, Sofia would have no qualms about telling her mother the whole truth. But Phil was her mother's sole priority now. She couldn't rely on her mother not to betray her trust and run to tell him everything.

The thought brought tears to her eyes. Her mother used to be the one person on this earth she would have trusted with any confidence. How drastically their relationship had been altered.

And Raul. To think that just a few hours ago, she'd thought they'd passed some kind of milestone. That he'd trusted her enough to be vulnerable in her presence. But he'd clammed up immediately after and now *this*.

Raul chose that moment to step onto the concrete patio. "Is everything all right? I saw you pacing."

She strode to him and held the phone up in answer.

CHAPTER TWELVE

FOR THE LIFE of him, Raul couldn't figure out how he kept messing up so badly when it came to Sofia.

What had started out as a carefree afternoon in heavenly surroundings had turned into yet another fiasco with pictures of them splashed all over the gossip sites. So much for camaraderie.

Now, as he sat next to her after dinner in the mayor's mansion, he wished he could get another opportunity to simply talk to her. Tell her that such moments were a matter of course in his life. He couldn't always control them. That sometimes he let his guard down—like absentmindedly taking his hat and glasses off in public during a heavy conversation—and the results were immediate. Like they had been at the botanical garden. Someone who happened to be paying attention had recognized him and snapped their photos. He wanted to tell her his actions had been careless but not intentional.

But they were about to be entertained by one of Canada's top sopranos during a private performance. Hardly the time or place to try to have any kind of useful conversation.

He stole a glance in her direction. In yet another gown that showed off all her stunning qualities. The color of her dress reminded him of the lilies they'd walked by yesterday. Creamy with a hint of subtle beige everywhere the fabric folded. Her hair was loose this evening, falling in thick, flowing waves over her shoulders. He'd asked back in DC if she wanted a stylist to travel with them. She'd said no and clearly didn't need one.

Raul scanned his gaze over the other guests. She was the subject of attention for most of the other males in attendance and she had been all night.

To the point where Raul had wanted to make up an excuse and leave with her before the appetizers were served. One particular guest, a poet here to receive an award for his latest political publication, was practically leering at her as he had for most of the night. Raul knew better but couldn't help but scowl, hoping the man would notice his displeasure. He did. Leaning back in his chair, he trained his eyes on the stage before them.

Finally, the lights dimmed in the small auditorium on the ground floor of the mansion and a petite woman in a toe-length black dress came on stage.

Sofia's gasp was audible as the woman began to sing. The Abarra family had always been patrons of the arts, and his mother had been an avid opera fan. But Raul didn't have the ear it took to appreciate what he was hearing. Clearly, Sofia did. She sat leaning forward in her chair, her jaw open, her eyes fixed on the woman singing. She most likely didn't even realize it but she'd grasped his hand on the armrest. As badly as he wanted to give it a squeeze, he didn't so much as move for fear she'd notice what she'd done and pull away.

Instead, he let her enjoy the performance, watching the artist, while he let himself enjoy watching *her*.

Finally after five songs that included a very challenging piece from *Madame Butterfly*, the singer took a bow. The audience roared with applause, everyone on their feet to deliver a standing ovation.

Sofia seemed to be the most boisterous of all with her cheering and clapping. When the lights rose again, she turned to him with glistening eyes. That telltale blush that tempted him so was back on her cheek.

"That was amazing," she said, her voice thick

and breathy. "What talent." She dabbed at her eyes, surprising him that she'd actually been brought to tears. "Thank you for such an opportunity."

He wanted to respond by hauling her to him and indulging in that kiss he couldn't stop thinking or dreaming about. The desire to taste her again was keeping him awake at night.

"I'm glad you enjoyed it, Sofia," he said, meaning it down to his very bones. A bittersweet sense of regret settled over him. This was it, the last event they were to be seen at together. After this she was to head back to DC and lay low for several days until speculation died down about their engagement. While he headed to the Laurentian Mountains for some much-needed rest and leisure before a slew of obligations that would keep him busy nonstop for the next several months. A quiet announcement would then be made by the royal assistant that the union hadn't worked out after all. The gossip outlets had already moved on from their focus on Luisa.

Mission accomplished.

So why did he feel such a crushing sense of disappointment, as if all the light was about to go out of his days?

They said their goodbyes after leaving the auditorium, thanking the mayor for her hospitality.

He turned to her when they were seated in

the back of the limousine. He had to get this off his chest.

"Look Sofia, I know our day at the gardens ended on a sour note. And I want to tell you that I'm deeply sorry." If his father could only hear him. The king of Vesovia and his sole heir were never expected to apologize to anyone outside of the royal family and a few select individuals on earth. But Raul knew what was right. "I should have been more thoughtful in preparing you for the possibility we might be recognized."

She smiled at him, the blue light of the interior throwing shadows over her beautiful features.

"Apology accepted," she said simply. No pouting, no angry glare or demand for further groveling like some of his previous liaisons might have done at the smallest slight.

She continued, moving him all the more. "And I should have been better about asking you to explain. I'd just been rather rattled by my mother's texts and reacted badly."

That was it then? They'd both apologized and cleared the air.

Was it really to be that simple?

It occurred to him then, a shocking realization that had his head spinning. Totally unexpected and paradigm shattering.

He was going to miss Sofia Nomi with every cell in his body.

* * *

Sofia still felt the rush of the performance she'd just experienced, such a melodic, haunting voice coming from such a small, angelic-looking woman. But if she were being honest with herself, she'd have to come to terms with the fact that her raw emotions had a lot to do with the man she'd been sitting next to all night. She would never tire of seeing the picture Raul made in his custom-tailored tuxedos.

This would be the last night she would see said picture. Hence the real reason for her charged state. By this time next week, their charade would be over and she'd be back home. More secure financially, a development she'd be forever grateful for. But sitting here in the back of a limousine with Raul's warmth and aftershave scent surrounding the air around her, she didn't feel much like celebrating her newfound wealth.

She may never see him again.

His apology just now had been nothing less than bittersweet. An apology she'd sincerely accepted because their time together was fast coming to a close. Plus, in his defense, she hadn't handled her emotions well after receiving those texts from her mother. So she'd lashed out as a result.

Apology or not, Raul was probably looking

forward to finally being rid of her and going back to his regular life. Unlike her.

The stinging in her eyes intensified and she bit down on her lip to keep real tears from forming. Her time with him was nothing more than a big pretense but how in the world would she be able to avoid comparing him to every other man she may meet?

Handsome and successful. He'd spoken fluent French with the mayor. They were there because the city was recognizing him as a major contributor to a Montreal-based charity that supported world refugees. He was everything a red-blooded woman could possibly want.

A man she could never have unless it was all a fantasy.

She couldn't avoid the sniffle no matter how hard she tried.

"Still feeling the effects of the performance then," he said, completely misunderstanding her emotional state.

"I guess so," she answered, forgiving herself for the small lie. "She was very talented."

"I know it's been a long evening and you must be tired, but I wondered if we may make a stop before heading back to the hotel."

As far as a distraction, a stop along the way wouldn't be unwelcome. "What kind of a stop?"

He smiled at her. "You'll see. Do you think you're up for it?"

She nodded in agreement. "I'm not tired at all."

"That's my princess," he said, sending a jolt of lightning through her core. She was no such thing in reality.

He pulled his cell phone out of his pocket and sent off a quick message. Within minutes, they were pulling up next to a well-lit square.

Raul left the car, then came around to the side to help her out. "Notre-Dame Basilica," he told her.

Sofia looked to the majestic fountain in front of one of the grandest structures she'd laid eyes on and uttered the only two words that came to mind, "Oh, my."

"Wait till you see the inside."

The square was empty except for the two of them, the hour rather late. "We can go inside?" she asked, unable to take her eyes off the marvel she was looking at.

"Technically it's closed to the public at this hour."

He didn't need to say the rest. Someone had obliged to open the doors for him.

He took her by the hand and walked her toward the entrance. When they made it inside, Sofia had to blink to make sure she wasn't seeing things. It was like stepping into a painting. It was a struggle trying to decide where to look. Long, intricately painted columns, with wood carved statues that decorated the high walls below a spangled ceiling that seemed to reach clear to the real night sky. All bathed in a crystal blue light that reminded her of the clear blue waters of the Caribbean Sea the one time she'd been there.

Everywhere she looked was a masterpiece of art.

She was speechless, could only stay rooted in her spot as her eyes took in all the splendor.

Finally, she found her voice. "Thank you for bringing me here. I'm glad I got to see this." The basilica was a wonderful place to end her trip.

Raul had been so thoughtful to set it up for her. The perfect parting gift.

It was past midnight by the time they arrived back at the hotel. Raul held the elevator door open for Sofia and waited as she stepped inside. He wasn't ready for the night to end just yet. Not when it was their last one together.

He was trying to come up with a way to ask her about a nightcap when her phone rang.

"It's Agnes," Sofia announced, her brow furled in concern. "Wonder why she's calling so late."

He waited while she answered. Agnes's faint voice came through the tiny speaker in a mumbled torrent, though Raul couldn't make out anything she was saying. Sofia didn't speak so much as a word. Her face grew ashen as she listened.

Raul clamped down on his impatience, resisting the urge to ask her what was wrong.

Finally, she hung up, her mouth slightly agape.

"Sofia? What is it?" he asked when he couldn't stand the suspense any longer.

Before answering, she tapped the screen of her phone several times. "See for yourself," she told him, handing him the device.

Raul was loath to tear his gaze away from her crestfallen face. When he finally did so to look at the screen, the reason for her upset was plain and clear.

"A hit piece."

She released a hysterical laugh. "On me. They're saying I'm an opportunist who has no business being engaged to a prince. A commoner who bathes animals for a living. That I'm taking advantage of your distraction with your sister to entrap you." Her voice grew higher in pitch as she spoke.

Raul bit out a curse, swearing at himself as much as at the worthless rag that had published such drivel. This was all his fault. If it wasn't for him, no one would even know who Sofia was let alone accuse her of such vile intentions.

Without thought, he stepped to her, drew her close.

"We'll handle this, Sofia. Get them to retract it. I'll get the palace press office on it right this minute."

She hiccupped. "But the damage has been done, hasn't it? The article is already out there."

He couldn't argue with her there. There was no erasing what had already found its way into cyberspace.

To his amazement, Sofia straightened in his arms and drew a deep breath. He could practically feel the strength she was summoning like some magical sprite calling upon the universe.

"But you're right," she began. "You said so yourself. Eventually they'll lose interest, won't they? This article will eventually be forgotten." The tremble in her voice sounded as if she were trying to convince herself more than looking for an answer.

He would have thought so. But now he wasn't so sure. This was all his fault. The things they were saying about Sofia, the accusations they were throwing at her. How could he not have seen it coming? Rather than viewing their engagement as a romantic love story, the media had turned their relationship into something nefarious and they'd painted Sofia as a villain in the process.

All because of him.

She wasn't sure how long she'd been out on the terrace when she heard the sliding door swish open. Raul stepped in front of her, still wearing his tuxedo. Sofia herself hadn't bothered to undress out of her gown, her mind still processing what the world was reading about her.

He handed her a steaming mug.

"You didn't have to make me a cup of tea," she said, taking the cup. "Thank you."

"You're welcome. Though I have a secondary motive."

"What would that be?"

"To make a suggestion and see what you think."

She studied him in the moonlight. He'd rammed his hand into his pant pockets. A muscle twitched along his jaw. He seemed uncharacteristically hesitant to say his next words.

"I know we've reached the end of our agreed-upon time."

Her mouth was dry, her mind scrambling to try to figure out where he was going with all this. "I'm aware."

"I know you have to keep a low profile for a

while until the spotlight on us falls, especially now. And I'll be off to Mont-Tremblant."

"Again, I'm aware," she repeated.

He tilted his head her way. "I think the media might be a bit more relentless than I first gave them credit for."

Sofia sighed and focused her attention on a twinkling star in the distant night sky. "I can handle it, Raul." What choice did she have? This was as much her fault as it was his. Neither one of them had thought to predict that at least one outlet would choose the most salacious and juicy angle.

He nodded. "I don't doubt it. But you shouldn't have to. Not by yourself."

"What does that mean?"

"Well, it occurred to me that there's no reason you have to wait out the media attention back home in DC."

Sofia scanned his face for any hint of what this conversation might really be about. He shocked her when he finally revealed the answer.

"Come with me, Sofia."

CHAPTER THIRTEEN

Mont-Tremblant, Canada

"Huh. I wouldn't have pegged a prince as the baking type."

Raul cut out a perfect square of the pastry he'd just pulled out of the refrigerator and plated it, handing it to Sofia with a dessert fork.

"Technically, I haven't. This is a no-bake dessert."

Sofia took a forkful and groaned in pleasure as she chewed. As much as he enjoyed her little sounds of delight and watching her enjoy her food, Raul had to look away. The temptation to replace that fork with his own lips was almost too strong to resist.

"How in the world did you learn to make these?" Sofia asked, a smidge of chocolate ganache smeared temptingly along her bottom lip.

"The sweet little old lady who owns the café in town took pity on me and gave me the recipe my last visit here. Guess she grew tired of me going by every day to buy out her entire case."

Sofia chuckled, took another bite of the Nanaimo bar, moaned again, louder this time.

She pointed the fork in his direction once she was done swallowing. "You're a man of many talents, Crown Prince Raul Abarra. But making these might be top of my list."

The pleasure he felt at the innocuous words was enough to be considered comically embarrassing. But that was the realization that kept repeating for him since they'd arrived here after leaving Montreal—pleasing Sofia was tremendously enjoyable for him. More gratifying than growing Vesovia's national investments, or appeasing the king. Or pretty much anything else he could think of.

And wasn't that a sorry state of affairs?

Considering none of this could last. In many ways, their stay here in the charming lodge he used as his base when he stayed in Mont-Tremblant was even more pretend than their fake engagement. Their days spent walking, hiking or shopping in the quaint town. Evenings spent side by side reading quietly. It was all so cozy. So domestic.

So opposite of what his real life actually entailed.

But looking at Sofia now, as she enjoyed her

dessert, the smile on her face while she savored every morsel, Raul couldn't bring himself to worry about the long term. Was it so wrong to enjoy the simplicity while it lasted? To pretend it didn't have to end?

When they finished eating, he followed her to the love seat in front of the fireplace.

"Are you going to pretend you intend on reading on your tablet again?" she asked, sitting down and curling her legs under her.

"Why, whatever do you mean?" he asked in mock confusion, though he knew full well what she was referring to.

She laughed, flipping open to her bookmarked page. "I mean that you always eventually lean over my shoulder to read my novel."

"Can't help it. Your whodunit is much more interesting than my boring spreadsheets of domestic supply chains."

She rubbed her chin. "Fair enough. Next time we're in town, we'll have to get you your own copy."

"Right. We should do that. Good idea."

He had absolutely no intention of doing any such thing. He had no idea what the plot was of the book she was reading, couldn't even name a character. The reason he sat next to her in the evenings and leaned into her shoulder had everything to do with how she smelled, the way she felt against him, the feel of her hair along his jaw.

Sometimes, as the evening grew later, he was lucky enough that she lost herself in the story and snuggled her back against his chest, let him wrap his arm around her.

He sat next to her now, then closed his tablet after less than ten minutes to lean over her shoulder.

She was, quite literally, near the top of the world. And high above ground.

Sofia took in the sights far below her feet dangling off the gondola car as it soared higher and higher along its line. A shimmering lake lay what seemed like miles below them. Lush green trees as far as the eye could see. Hiking trails that meandered down the slope. The populous town at the base of the mountain appeared like one of those miniature village models that hobby enthusiasts put together.

"I feel like I'm flying," she said on a laugh.

Raul flashed her a charming smile in response. She was referring to more than just the gondola ride. In the week since they'd left Montreal, she felt like she'd been bouncing on clouds.

Who knew she was so adventurous? So far they'd been kayaking, hiking and had slid down a synthetic luge path.

Raul certainly took his leisure time seriously. And she was so very happy to be along for the ride. The fantasy had been unexpectedly extended, and she wasn't going to overthink the unfortunate turn of events that had led her here.

Maybe accepting Raul's invitation hadn't been wise. She could have just as well hunkered down in her mom's apartment in DC, staying out of sight until the world forgot about her. But her heart would have felt empty, a hole in her life where Raul had once been.

And if she was delaying the inevitable, then so be it. Nothing would make her regret the two weeks she'd spent here in the mountains with him. Adding more days to the cherished memories she'd made in Raul's company was nothing less than a gift.

"When we come back sometime in the winter, we'll be skiing down this mountain," Raul said now loudly above the sound of the wind.

Sofia didn't trust her balance, coordination or ski skills enough to be excited about that statement. But one word he'd used caught her attention and did send a thrill down her spine.

When.

She'd lost count of the times back in Toronto and Montreal when she'd longed for Raul to hint that he might be with her on a future trip to someplace exciting. Who knew? Maybe they'd make it back to all the places on her mental travel list together after all.

They reached the top of the mountain and jumped off the car. The air felt different up here. Crisper, more energizing. And the view was one of a kind.

"Now the fun part," Raul said, guiding her by the elbow. "We hike all the way down."

It was all tremendous fun as far as she was concerned. Sofia leaned down to tighten the laces on the special boots they'd purchased in town upon their arrival. Raul had the whole trip planned with a full schedule of activities from morning till night. Today's agenda might be the most challenging yet.

She'd known Raul was athletic and fit, but the lengths to which he drove himself simply to have some fun was exhausting to watch and impossible to keep up with.

"I'm afraid I'm going to end up slowing you down on our descent," she told him when she rose.

He tapped her playfully on the nose. "All that matters is the journey."

They appeared to be the only two people on the mountaintop. Threatening clouds had been approaching from the west but a check and re-check of the weather had assured them any pending storm would pass by the mountain entirely.

Looking in that direction now, Sofia actually crossed her fingers in hopes that was true. The sky looked awful dark out that way.

"Let's go, shall we?" Raul prompted.

They'd only made it down a few feet when Sofia's finger crossing proved futile. Within moments the sky turned dark. All those angry clouds had indeed found their way above the summit and unleashed a torrent of rain.

Raul swore next to her. "I guess the weather reports were wrong. I blame myself for trusting them blindly."

Sofia wanted to offer words of reassurance that he couldn't possibly blame himself for an unexpected shift in rain clouds, but she was too busy getting soaked.

"Here, let's try to find some shelter," he told her, wiping his face and looking around. "Most of the trails have small cottages for hikers to take a break or if they need first aid."

It was almost impossible to see. As high up as they were, the wind was surprisingly strong. Sofia actually wondered if she might tip over.

"I think I see one," Raul said finally.

She could only follow him blindly, making sure her hand remained in his. After several difficult steps with the ground beneath them getting muddier and muddier, they finally reached a small wooden shedlike structure nestled between two tall trees.

It certainly wasn't much. To call it any kind of cottage would be overselling it.

The door swung open and crashed against the wall when Raul pushed it open.

"Looks like this one isn't used anymore," he said once they'd stepped inside and shut the door behind them.

"It works," she replied. "All that matters is it has a roof."

"I'm so sorry, Sofia," Raul said, his features tight. "It's no wonder we appear to be the only ones on this mountain."

She stepped closer, laid a hand on his forearm. "You only have a few days free." He'd even left his bodyguards behind on this trip, explaining to her that every time he'd been to Mont-Tremblant, no one had cared who he was or what he was doing. This place was like another world, set apart from the rest. "It's understandable you didn't want to miss out on one. And I'm also an adult—I had just as much responsibility for the decision."

His eyes scanned her face and Sofia's breath hitched in her throat. Sometimes when he looked at her that way, she wanted to curl her fingers through his hair and bring his mouth down to hers for a deep, satisfying kiss.

"You're shivering," he said, his voice a low whisper she almost didn't hear above the loud wind outside.

She may be soaked and cold, but any trembling happening at the moment was his doing. "Am I?"

He stepped closer. "You are. We might have to see about keeping you warm."

She could think of a few ways to do that where he'd be the primary operative in the endeavor.

Sofia swallowed as he stepped even closer. They were a hairbreadth apart now, and his breath felt warm on her cheek. He was so wrong about her feeling cold. Right now she felt nothing but singeing heat from the bottom of her feet to the top of her head. And everything in between.

"Would you like me to get you warm, Sofia?"

Much, much too late for the question. He already had her burning up. "Yes," she answered, surprised her tongue worked. "I would like that very much."

She barely got the last word out before his mouth was on hers. His arms wound about her waist, lifting her slightly off the ground. The taste of him was intoxicating, overwhelming her senses. She'd wanted this for so long, dreamed of it during the nights. Woke up yearning for him in the mornings. Finally. Blessedly.

All thought fled her mind. The only thing her brain registered was the feel of him against her, the taste of him. His scent surrounding her.

Her hand found its way into his shirt; feeling the hard muscle against her palm sent her desire soaring even higher. As did his responding groan.

Her other hand plunged into the hair at his neck and she pulled him closer, deeper.

Suddenly, abruptly the kiss was over. Raul tore his mouth off hers and yanked himself back.

Sofia could only blink in shock and disappointment. They both stood panting for several silent moments. She stepped toward him and he held a hand up to stop her.

The rejection came as a swift blow to her midsection. What had just happened? How could he stop so suddenly? And why? Had she thrown herself at him? How humiliating. She felt a flush rush to her face at the possibility.

She couldn't find the words to ask.

"Not like this," he said finally, his voice gravelly and thick.

Her confusion must have been clear on her face.

He leaned closer, trailed a finger down her cheek. "You can't think I don't want you." He sucked in a deep breath, squeezed his eyes shut.

"But when this happens, it won't be in a dingy abandoned shack." There was that word again.

When.

He opened his eyes again and stared straight into her soul, then he dropped a gentle kiss to her temple. "And it won't be rushed and thoughtless. You won't feel soaked to the skin with rainwater. I'll make sure you feel nothing but pure pleasure. Over and over."

Hours later, once the storm ended and they finally made their way back to the lodge, he stayed true to his word.

He'd broken every one of his rules when it came to Sofia. The sun was just rising when he felt her up against him, rustling in her sleep. Raul willed her not to wake up just yet. He didn't know what to say to her.

He didn't regret what happened between them last night. But that didn't mean he had no misgivings. For one, he should have been clearer up front about exactly what last night meant in case she had any misconstrued ideas. He should have explained that he wasn't the right man for her. That there would be a spotlight on her at all times if she were to become involved with him romantically. Living that life might have been manageable for her for a few days of pretend, but long term was a completely different story.

As if that weren't bad enough, he had no time in his life for any kind of real relationship. The kingdom was always going to take up most of his time and energy. Which would only be a bigger factor once he actually ascended the throne. His father made it more and more clear with each passing day that he was getting ready to hand the proverbial reins over to Raul.

Sofia had a life she'd worked hard for. With the amount he'd transferred into her bank account for her assistance with Luisa's mess, Sofia wouldn't have to worry about budgeting or making ends meet in her shop. She lived in a city she loved with supportive friends and her mother nearby.

How could he ask her to give up all that for him?

He couldn't. The fact of the matter was that when he did finally settle down, it most likely wouldn't be for love. It would be for duty to the kingdom with a woman who had been raised to fit into such a life. He'd be fooling himself to think otherwise for even a moment.

Look at the havoc the attention on her had caused just for the brief time they'd pretended to be engaged. How could he ask her to deal with that for the rest of her life? She couldn't and didn't have to.

All of that should have been laid out in the

open with Sofia before he'd acted on his urges and complicated everything.

He swore. In fact, even asking her here to Mont-Tremblant with him was a mistake. The first time in his life he'd acted on a whim. Driven by unplanned impulse. He couldn't even explain what had gotten into him the night of the mayoral dinner when he'd taken her to the basilica. He simply recalled that one moment he was looking forward to coming here alone, just to unwind after all that had taken place these last few weeks. The next, he couldn't bear the thought of being here without her.

Then he'd compounded the errors by not being up front with Sofia before they became intimate. He could only hope the damage wouldn't be irreparable.

She must have just missed him. Sofia awoke to find Raul's side of the bed still warm but he was nowhere to be found. It was no wonder she'd slept through his awakening this morning. Nothing less than an earthquake would have roused her after such an eventful day. And what came after later at night. Being stranded in a little shack on the side of a deserted mountain sounded like something out of one of those romantic movies Agnes was so fond of.

Her friend would never believe she'd actually lived such a storyline. Complete with the romantic interlude it had led to. With a satisfied stretch, she reached for her phone on the bedside table. He'd left her a message. Nothing from her mom, which was what she'd asked of her. But a conflicting mash of disappointment and relief washed over her that her mother hadn't tried harder to reach her after the botanical garden photos.

The only message she'd received was from Raul.

Out running on one of the mountain trails. See you soon.

A twinge of disappointment nagged at her at the straightforward message. No heart emoji or xoxo.

But that was silly. Most men didn't really do such things, did they? After all, this wasn't really a romance movie.

Honestly, how did the man have any energy to run after last night? She could barely move a muscle and felt loath to so much as get out of bed. But a cup of coffee was called for and the sun was shining bright outside. No time like right now to start the day. Plus, she was feeling rather like a relative underachiever given Raul was already out and about and strenuously exercising.

Making her way to the kitchen, she approached the newfangled coffee contraption she was just recently getting the hang of. Making quick work of drinking the first one, she brewed a second to enjoy on the stone patio outside. The morning had only grown brighter since she'd risen.

Her coffee cup was halfway empty when Raul showed up. Dressed in a tight T-shirt that stuck to him with sweat, accentuating the toned muscles of his chest. Sofia's heart fluttered with awareness at the sight of him.

Standing, she strode the few feet to where he stood and leaned in, intending a good-morning kiss. Raul stepped back slightly but enough for her to notice, then landed a chaste peck on the side of her cheek.

An unpleasant sensation slithered down her spine.

"I'm pretty sweaty," he said by way of explanation.

She was about to reply that she didn't mind but the hardened lines around his lips and the tension in his shoulders had alarm bells ringing in her head. She saw no hint of the affectionate, passionate man she'd spent last night with. Did he regret what had happened between them last night?

The thought sent a stab of pain through her center.

Don't jump to conclusions.

Maybe he was just tired from his run.

She summoned a bright smile. "So, last full day here in Mont-Tremblant." she said just to get some kind of conversation going.

"That's right," he said. "Then it's back to reality."

She was going to ignore whatever hidden meaning such a statement might hold. "Well, as much as I miss DC and everyone back there, including Sir Bunbun, I think you've awakened the traveler in me."

He lifted an eyebrow. "Oh?"

She nodded. "That's right. I'm already planning a trip back to Toronto. I never did get to the top of the CN Tower."

He nodded once. "I remember. I think it's a great idea. You should go."

You. Not *we.*

Maybe she was being foolish, masochistic even, but she had to ask and know for sure what was happening at the moment. Though she knew she was about to risk shattering her heart. "What does your calendar look like coming up? I'd love some company."

"I don't think that would be such a good idea, Soso. I should head back to Vesovia and stay still for a while. I've been away quite long."

A brick dropped to the pit of her stomach. Not only at his words, but the reversion back to the teasing nickname he'd used for her when she'd been nothing more to him than his younger sister's pesky little friend.

Still, her heart wouldn't let her accept what her mind was clearly registering. "Oh. That makes sense. Well, I've always wanted to see your kingdom. Vesovia attracts a lot of tourists this time of year, doesn't it? Maybe I could venture out there for a quick visit."

He shook his head with zero hesitation. "I don't think that would work either."

That settled it. There was no denying now what was standing in front of her nose. He was washing his hands of her. While last night had meant the world to her, apparently Raul had merely been indulging in a last-minute fling before they each went back to their own lives.

How utterly stupid and naive of her that she hadn't even considered that possibility. After all, he'd never told her anything to the contrary. Why in the world had she assumed that one night meant anything genuine?

Because it had for her. Because she'd fallen in love with him.

While he was ready to simply walk away from her and not look back.

CHAPTER FOURTEEN

FOR THE SECOND time in a month, a royal Abarra from the Kingdom of Vesovia entered Sofia's grooming shop without any kind of advance warning. Princess Luisa was beautiful as ever, sporting a golden tan and her usual mischievous smile.

Any other time, Sofia would have been thrilled to see her friend. But her first reaction upon Luisa's arrival was how much she wished the other sibling were here in her stead.

Luisa didn't bother with a hello, just launched into conversation as if her showing up here wasn't a complete anomaly.

"I heard you and my brother had some kind of fling. Only it wasn't real. Except maybe it was."

Well, that was quite a greeting. "What are you doing here, Luisa? And why didn't you tell me you were coming?"

The princess gave a dismissive wave of her hand. "Because it was a spontaneous decision."

Par for the course.

"That answers one of my questions."

"Well, older bro has been an absolute monster lately. Grouchy, grumpy. Seems miserable in general. I wanted to know if you were the cause of his sudden nasty disposition."

Sofia rolled her eyes at the question. "I hardly think so. He was probably working on some deal for the kingdom's coffers that fell through."

Luisa shook her head, tightening her lips. "No, I don't think that's it. He's dealt with unsuccessful deals before. What he hasn't dealt with before is lost love."

Sofia couldn't bring herself to take Luisa's words seriously. And she would absolutely ignore that last word because it didn't fit.

Raul had been very clear that last morning at Mont-Tremblant. He wanted nothing to do with her once the trip was over. Whatever Luisa thought she knew, she was sorely mistaken.

"Be that as it may," she began, "I don't want to talk about your brother. I'd like to talk about you, however. You caused quite a stir for several weeks there."

Luisa gave a disaffected shrug of one elegant shoulder. "Yes, I suppose I did. I made some bad decisions and fell for a man who said all the right things but went right back to his wife when the time came to make a decision."

Sofia could certainly relate to part of that scenario. She'd made her fair share of bad decisions over the past few weeks and she'd undoubtedly fallen for the wrong man.

Luisa leaned over her counter. "But we have to talk about big bro," she declared. "It's why I'm here. He's becoming unbearable. Someone has to do something. My guess is that someone is you."

Why was Luisa not getting it? She meant nothing to Raul. She couldn't fix something she had no effect over.

Agnes chose that moment to rush out from the back office. "I've booked our tickets, Sofia." She came to a halt when she saw the princess and blinked twice. Luisa definitely didn't fit the example of their regular clientele. She looked like... Well, she looked like a royal princess in a small pet groomer shop.

Sofia made quick introductions while Agnes continued to stare at the out-of-place specimen who'd clearly honored them with her mere presence.

"Tickets to where?" Luisa wanted to know.

"Toronto," Agnes blurted out before she got a chance to answer. "We're going together in three weeks. She's been talking about returning there for another visit since she got back to DC a month ago."

Luisa tilted her head in question.

"I never got to the top of the CN Tower," Sofia said, not sure why she was bothering. She didn't really owe Luisa any kind of explanation. In fact, if it wasn't for the princess, her heart would still be intact in her chest instead of shattered into a billion pieces.

Her antics had set the entire disaster in motion.

Suddenly, her patience had grown thin and her ire not so much. "Luisa, I'm really busy. Can we please get on with the real reason you're here already?"

Luisa's eyes widened in surprise. Sofia had never so much as said a harsh word to her before. Not many people had. Maybe it was about time that changed.

"I already told you."

"And I told you that makes zero sense. Follow me, please."

This time Luisa's jaw actually snapped open in shock. Now Sofia was literally ordering her around. But she didn't really care at the moment. She'd worked hard to begin the long journey of trying to piece her heart back together. So far she hadn't been terribly successful but Luisa's sudden appearance was picking the scabs of what little progress she'd made.

Without waiting for the princess to agree, Sofia turned on her heel and made her way to the back office. They were in between clients and her two new employees had asked for the day off, apparently to go on a date with each other.

There were only the three of them in the shop. She was rather surprised to turn around and find that the princess had, in fact, heeded her demand as she was standing in the room behind her.

She moved behind her desk and sat, motioning for Luisa to take the other chair. "I don't know what your brother told you—"

Luisa cut her off. "He didn't tell me anything. He's barely talked to me, still angry about what he calls my poor behavior and judgment."

"Maybe he's right."

"Of course he is. What's that got to do with anything?"

Sofia rubbed her forehead where a small headache was beginning.

"Luisa, I don't know what you came here expecting to get but I can't give it to you."

"I beg to differ," she said, plopping into the chair. "Did you even ask him?"

"Ask him what?"

"Ask him how he felt about you."

Sofia couldn't find the words to even respond.

"You need to ask him. And soon. He can hardly run the kingdom in the state he's in."

That did it. Of all the selfish, non-self-aware outlooks to have. "Well, then maybe *you* should step up. You're also a royal. Why is Vesovia's well-being dependent solely on Raul?"

If she'd shocked Luisa before, the princess was downright gobsmacked now. Narrowing her eyes, she stood back up and walked to the door. "Just ask him," she said, leaving the office.

"Wait!" Sofia called to her retreating back. Maybe she'd been too harsh just now but her nerves were still too raw and Luisa had never really had to answer for her often selfish behavior before. The princess was past due to hear a few truths. "You came all the way to Washington. Do you want to at least get lunch or something?"

Luisa didn't bother to turn around or so much as slow her stride. "Sure," she answered over her shoulder. "I'll have my staff call you when it's arranged."

With that she was gone.

Sofia wasn't going to hold her breath waiting on that lunch.

Leaning back in the chair, she let her head hang over the back. She felt utterly drained by Luisa's stealth visit. But as haughty and impulsive as she could be, Luisa had always been sharp as a tack. And her read of people wasn't often wrong. Especially of those people she considered loved ones.

What he hasn't dealt with before is lost love

* * *

Married life certainly seemed to suit his friend. Raul took in his friend's relaxed shoulders and wide smile and felt a pang of envy before pushing it aside. Rafe had gone to the trouble of stopping by Vesovia to see him on his way from their honeymoon and Raul owed it to him to be somewhat personable. And not a grouchy ogre as Luisa accused him of being. She was wrong of course. Raul wasn't grouchy. He was simply busy.

He turned back to his friend as one of the kitchen staff refilled their wineglasses while they dined on the terrace adjacent to the royal gardens. "And how is your lovely new bride," he asked. "Was Frannie not able to accompany you?"

"Afraid not," Rafe answered with a frown. "She had to leave right away to film on location in Hawaii."

"You miss her already," Raul said. It didn't take a magician to see what was clearly written on his friend's face.

"Like a limb," Rafe answered, a faraway look in his eyes.

His friend had it bad. At least Rafe knew he'd be reunited with the woman he was in love with.

Whoa. Raul stopped short. That wayward

thought had no business scurrying around in his brain.

Raul set his glass down and stared out into the acres and acres of green grass and shrubbery. He avoided coming out here most days. The view reminded him too much of the botanical garden, which in turn reminded him of Sofia.

All she'd asked for was a simple visit. Not unlike what Rafe was here for. And he'd coldly turned her down. He hadn't even tried to come up with a way to explain why.

She must think him a selfish, callous ass.

"So where'd you just drift off to?" Rafe asked, amusement dancing in his eyes. "I must say, I don't think I've ever seen you this distracted. You still thinking about your split?"

He really must have drifted off. Raul had no idea what Rafe was referring to. "Split?"

Rafe nodded. "Yeah. I was sorry to hear things didn't work out between you and Sofia," Rafe said. "Frannie and I really enjoyed her at the wedding. May I ask what led to the breakup? You can tell me to mind my own business if you prefer not to talk about it."

Up until hearing those words, Raul was certain he indeed did not want to talk about it. But instead of saying just that, he found himself spilling the entirety of his and Sofia's now-defunct arrangement, ending with an apology for misleading him and Frannie and at their wedding, no less.

Rafe blew out a long whistle, studying him. "But you asked her to go with you to the mountains." Funny, he hadn't so much as acknowledged the rest of the sordid tale. Or his apology, for that matter.

"Right. I should have never done that. Sofia deserves stability. A life of quiet, away from prying eyes and cameras. I can't give her that. My fate lies in marriage to a woman who's familiar with the pressure and unwanted attention that being part of the royal family requires. I should have been better at explaining all that to her."

"I don't think that's it," Rafe countered before he'd had so much as a chance to finish the sentence.

"Of course it is."

Rafe shook his head. "Man, you're one of the most levelheaded people I know. A true future king who'll do well by his people. I have no doubt."

"Why do I sense a huge 'however' about to drop my way?" Raul said around a groan of resignation.

Rafe flashed him a smile. "Bingo. Give the man a prize. The 'however' happens to be that I think you've just come up with an excuse to walk away. Because the real truth is that you're scared."

Raul could only laugh in response to the preposterous statement.

Rafe continued, "Look it's understandable. You had to step up before you were ready. I get it. The king checked out because of his grief. I respect and admire your father but you know that's the truth.

Raul shrugged. "What's that got to do with me supposedly being scared? Or with Sofia for that matter?"

Rafe leaned back in his chair with a long sigh. "Guess I'm going to have to spell it out.

"Please do."

"You're scared of becoming vulnerable. Because you saw what became of your father when he lost the love of his life. And you can't bring yourself to risk the same fate happening to you. As for Sofia, I think you know how what I'm saying concerns her."

The view was just as spectacular as Raul had said. Sofia stood on the observation deck of the CN Tower watching the sparkling lights of Toronto rotate almost fifteen hundred feet below.

The scene was breathtaking really. Everything she'd imagined and more. So it made no sense that she wasn't standing here full of excitement and wonder.

In fact, she was miserable.

As great a travel companion as Agnes was, being up here felt off. Wrong somehow. Because even after the devastating morning on that patio in Mont-Tremblant, her misbehaving imagination had still insisted on conjuring him by her side whenever she pictured herself here.

All these weeks later and that sad fact hadn't changed.

Coming here was a mistake. It only served to remind her what she couldn't have. More accurately, who she couldn't have. She felt the stinging behind her eyes she thought had finally abated. Coming to the top of the tower was supposed to bring her closer. This trip was supposed to show her that she was fine without him. That she was ready to move on.

Who was she kidding? Sofia was far from fine.

She was sad and heartbroken and confused.

The ache of loneliness in her heart grew heavier with each passing day. No trip to the top of a tower was going to help heal that ache.

There was only one remedy that might.

She had to get some answers. She had to know once and for all if Raul had felt even a smidgeon of the way she felt.

If he'd grown to love her the way she'd fallen in love with him. Staring at the glimmering city below her now, she realized the trip to Toronto had been her way of delaying what was clearly inevitable.

Once and for all, she had to find out if any of it was real. As much as she begrudged to admit it, Luisa was right. She had to ask him.

Even if his answer shattered her heart for good and forever. That was a risk she was going to have to take.

Agnes appeared by her side after her latest stroll around the deck. Sofia forced a fake smile on her lips. The last thing she wanted was to mar the trip she'd talked her friend into taking with her.

"I could stay here all day and look at this skyline all night," Agnes said, clasping her hands in front of her in excitement.

Sofia couldn't bring herself to lie. She'd had enough of the view that should have brought her nothing but delight. "I think I've had enough. For tonight, I mean. We should definitely come back tomorrow." Which she would suck up and do it if that's what Agnes wanted.

"All right. But how about a quick drink in the pub downstairs first?"

Sofia really didn't have it in her, but she didn't have the heart to turn her friend down. Especially considering she was cutting the night short for both of them.

"Sure," she answered, following Agnes to the elevator. The pub was fairly empty when they made their way in. The night was relatively young still. Most tourists were out exploring or on the observation deck they'd just left. They headed to one of the empty tables in the corner.

Sofia ordered a glass of cabernet while Agnes went for the chilled ice wine Canada was known for, much sweeter than what Sofia was in the mood for. In fact, nothing about her mood felt any way sweet at the moment.

The waiter was back soon after taking their order but the drink he put down in front of her was most certainly not red wine.

"I think there's been some sort of mistake," she told the man, who had confirmed her order when he'd first taken it. "This isn't what I asked for."

She was expecting an apology and to be told that it was a simple mistake. Instead, the waiter shrugged. "Yeah, there's a gentleman that told the bartender you might want to try this first."

Sofia's radar triggered. Having strangers send a woman drinks was suspicious to say the least. Particularly when traveling. But then she realized why the cocktail looked familiar. The waiter confirmed her suspicion. "It's called the Caesar,"

he said, then added, "But I can take it back if
you want."

Agnes sat watching the exchange, confusion
clear in her chocolate brown eyes. "Sofia, what's
going on?"

She wasn't sure, but she was beginning to sus-
pect who might have sent the drink over. Her
pulse pounded under her skin, while her heart
thumped like a jackhammer under her rib cage,
then threatened to explode right out of her chest
when Raul appeared from the corner of the darkened room.

But it couldn't be him. She had to be seeing
things.

Sofia blinked and rubbed at her eyes just to
be sure.

"Do you want to send the drink back then?"
the waiter asked, sounding impatient.

"No, thank you. I'll keep it."

Agnes followed the direction of her gaze, then
stiffened when she saw Raul. He was at their
table a moment later.

"Wha-what are you doing here?" she asked
him.

Agnes shot her a questioning look. She answered with a nod that it was okay. She got up
and walked to a nearby table, taking her glass
of ice wine.

"Fine, but I'll be right here. Watching," she

yelled out in warning rather loudly before taking the chair.

For the life of her she couldn't figure out what to say. So she blurted the first thing that came to mind. "You don't look like a grouchy ogre." She wanted to suck the words back in as soon as they left her mouth.

In fact, he looked heart-shatteringly handsome. The dark eyes she'd missed so much. Those toned and muscular forearms below another shirt with rolled-up sleeves.

After an initial look of surprise at her statement, he threw his head back and laughed.

"Why are you here, Raul?"

He crouched down in front of her, taking both her hands in his own. "I'm here because I heard you would be."

"Luisa told you." She stated the obvious.

He nodded. "That's right. And I didn't want to spend another moment without you. Even though it's so unfair for me to ask that of you."

"Unfair how?"

"You will never know true privacy or anonymity ever again if you're with me. Articles like the one Agnes warned you about are sure to be written again. And again."

Sofia swallowed. The strain and concern in his voice as he spoke tugged at her heart. Concern for her. "I see."

"But I promise to do all that I can to make it all right. I'll be by your side, or we can simply go into hiding. I can try to rule from the Laurentian Mountains. Whatever you want. If you'll have me."

She shook her head, unable to quite believe what she was hearing. It was so hard to find the right words. She scrambled to try the best she could. "I don't care about running from cameras. I don't care if I have to duck paparazzi or curious bystanders for the rest of my life. All of that is worth it and more to be with you."

"That makes me the luckiest man on the planet," he said, his voice thick. "Because, somewhere along the way, when I wasn't paying attention, I fell deeply in love with you."

That settled it. She was definitely imagining all this. The air must have been too thin when she'd been up in the tower. The only explanation that made sense. Her mind was delirious due to a lack of sufficient oxygen.

She reached out to his face. If he was a ghost of her imagination, she should touch nothing but air. But her fingertips felt warm, solid flesh. He turned to drop a kiss inside her palm. The feel of his lips sent waves of hot electricity through her entire body.

"Oh, Raul. I've fallen in love with you too. Hopelessly, madly in love."

He sucked in a gasp of a breath at her words. Then, silently, he reached inside his pocket. Sofia clasped a hand to her mouth when she saw what he held.

"You left this behind," he told her, opening the small velvet box.

The beautiful ring her finger had grown so familiar wearing sat on a fluffy bed of satin. It was even lovelier than she remembered.

"Sofia Nomi. I'm a fool who doesn't deserve you and I know if you say yes, life as you know it will change forever. But I'm asking you to marry me." He paused to suck in a breath. "Please say yes."

She didn't need words to give him the answer he'd asked for.

EPILOGUE

SOFIA KNOCKED SOFTLY on the door to her husband's office and didn't wait for an answer before pushing it open. He'd been working since early morning and could use the break. Besides, she had some rather important news she had to tell him.

Raul glanced at his watch after flashing her a smile of greeting. Even after all these months, his smile sent a wave of longing through her. She couldn't resist taking a moment to stride behind his desk and lean in for a toe-curling kiss.

"Is it time to meet the king for lunch already?" he asked, then yanked her onto his lap. "I'm sure he won't mind if we're a little late," he added, taking her mouth with his once again.

Sofia lost focus as she reveled in the taste of him. Trailing her hands up his chest then around his neck, she pulled him closer and allowed herself to fully savor him. Then made herself pull away, though it wasn't easy. At this rate, she was never going to get the announcement out.

"No, it's early still," she said, breathless with happiness and the effects of the kiss. "There's another reason I'm here."

He lifted an eyebrow. "What reason?"

"I wanted to let you know about a new addition to the palace."

Raul flashed her an indulgent smile. "An addition, huh? Let me guess, we've adopted another cat from the shelter. What does that bring the number up to? Six? Seven? I've lost count."

She shook her head, hardly able to keep herself from just blurting out the news. She'd been floating on air since leaving her appointment with the palace nurse half an hour ago.

"Uh-uh. Wrong guess, my love."

He dropped a kiss to her forehead. "Another puppy then? Or a senior dog. We'll have to expand the kennels at this rate and hire another caretaker for them all."

"Wrong again."

"Oh, no. Not more bunnies. Those creatures seem to be multiplying enough on their own."

She gave another shake of her head. "You are wrong on all counts. And out of guesses."

He tilted his head in question.

She couldn't resist dropping another kiss to

his lips before continuing. "This particular addition is one of the two-legged variety."

Raul's eyes grew wide and his jaw fell open. Shock flooded his eyes but it didn't last, immediately replaced with joy. And love. Pure unfiltered love.

With a whoop loud enough that the entire palace must have heard, he stood up out of the chair and lifted her in his arms.

"You mean…?"

She nodded, laughter bursting from her throat. "Yes!"

He twirled her around, then lowered her to the ground to hug her tight. Sofia mentally paused to simply savor this moment in time. That night at the CN Tower, Raul had said he was the luckiest man on earth. She was pretty lucky herself to have found him.

Her prince had given her all she could have dared to hope for. And more.

Who knew fairy tales could sometimes be real?

* * * * *

If you enjoyed this story,
check out these other great reads from
Nina Singh

Bound by the Boss's Baby
Their Accidental Marriage Deal
Part of His Royal World
The Prince's Safari Temptation

All available now